CAST T...

There was a l...
edge of the wood... ...s, and the
hunting party em... ...brandishing all manner
of rifles. . . .

I tossed Ginny and Dalliance into the snow
and made for what was left of the old chimney,
the only cover close to me.

I looked back at Dally. She and the kid were
up and running toward the woods away from
the rifle gang.

The shooting was ripping up the air.

I slipped a half-brick out of the chimney
rubble and hefted it. I used to chuck rocks at
rats in the county dump back home when I was
a kid. I could snap one at fifty paces.

I heaved my brick through the air and it
beaned one guy good. He went down. The others set off more gunfire. . . .

PRAISE FOR PHILLIP DePOY AND *EASY*

"Easy is populated with wildly
appealing characters and
an unusually engaging detective."
—*The Independent Reader*

"A must read for fans of a down-home
mystery."
—Harriet Klausner, *Painted Rock Reviews*

ALSO BY PHILLIP DEPOY

Easy

Too Easy

Messages from Beyond

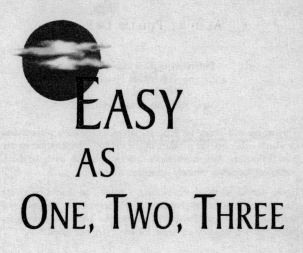

EASY
AS
ONE, TWO, THREE

Phillip DePoy

A DELL BOOK

Published by Dell Publishing
a division of Random House, Inc.
1540 Broadway
New York, New York 10036

ISBN: 0-440-22617-1

Printed in the United States of America

Published simultaneously in Canada

February 1999

Design by Kathryn Parise

10 9 8 7 6 5 4 3 2 1

OPM

CONTENTS

Contents

EASY
AS
ONE, TWO, THREE

LOST PINES

You see a ghost in the middle of the road. Naturally there's a full moon. Just how are you supposed to handle *that*? I was told it was exactly midnight on old Route 27. The hands of the clock were pressed straight up—like hands in prayer. The little girl seemed to just *appear* in the high beams of the Chevy. She was all dressed up in a bright red jumpsuit. The truck swerved to miss her and ended up in the McDonner corn patch. Mustard Abernathy and his pregnant wife, Sissy, were miraculously unharmed. Maybe it was on account of those praying clock hands on the dashboard.

Mustard put out his big old arm. "Hon?"

Sissy blew out a sizable breath. "I'm okay." Felt her stomach. "Baby's okay."

They both looked back to the road. It was empty. Mustard got out and looked for ten minutes, but there was no trace of the little girl in red. She was gone like smoke.

He had it in mind to hunt farther down the road. He was certain he saw some moonlit shadows moving in the ditch, but Sissy called out to him, "Sugar? I believe this baby's ready."

Mustard hustled back to the truck, tore up more of Mr. McDonner's corn patch, and peeled out to the hospital. Within the hour there was a new Baby Girl Abernathy in Stone County, and Sissy was fast asleep. Mustard was watching the late-night news. It was a story about Saint Patrick's Day in Savannah, Georgia—home of the biggest parade of its ilk outside of New York City.

Mustard leaned forward to make sure he recognized the face on the screen, then touched Sissy's shoulder. "Sweetie, your cousin Dalliance is on the TV."

Sissy went right on sleeping, but Mustard watched the rest of the item, even turned the sound up a little.

The reporter was interviewing the owner of the very popular nightspot Easy Two on River Street in Savannah.

"Would you say this was the largest crowd you'd ever had at your club, Ms. Oglethorpe?"

Dalliance Oglethorpe was not ever a big one for hyperbole. "It's a large crowd all right, but this is our first Saint Patrick's Day, so I've really got nothing to compare it to. I understand it's more or less *always* like this on Saint Patrick's Day around here."

The newscaster peered back into the camera.

"There you have it, Phil, the largest crowd ever. I'm Melissa Tynan, reporting from River Street."

The next story was about rampant bungling in Cobb County government, so Mustard turned off the set—didn't want to disturb Sissy's sleep.

Now, me, I'm not a big believer in ghost stories—or in Saint Patrick's Day, when it comes to it. I'm a big believer in memories in place of ghosts, and in saints that really did something, like Brendan, maybe—and in Dalliance Oglethorpe, the finest pal a guy ever had. I asked her once how she'd gotten such a name. Said it had something to do with the transitory nature of love—or at least the brevity of the relationship between her mother and her father. But I digress.

I only meant to explain that I was not the least bit upset when the phone woke me up at four in the morning on March eighteenth.

"Hello?"

"Flap? You asleep?"

"Dally?"

"Aunt Dally to you."

"Aunt Dally? Too Old South. Sorry. Can't say it."

She giggled. "No, I mean I just got a call from my cousin up in Stone County. I'm an aunt."

I tried to be enthusiastic. "Hey. That's something." Tried to sit up. "But if it's your cousin, aren't you a great-aunt or a second aunt or something?"

"Oh, I'll be great at it, all right." She had to talk over the noise where she was. "Look, I'm coming home tomorrow. Meet me about . . . one? Late lunch. We'll take a little drive up north."

"Don't want to."

"Sure you do. And a happy Saint Patrick's to you."

"Is it *that* time of year again already?"

Somebody jostled her and knocked the phone out of her hand. By the time she retrieved it, I was nodding off again.

She talked too loud. "Are you going to meet me or not?"

I sighed. "Majestic?"

"I feel like vegetables. Let's go to Mary Mac's."

"Uh-huh." Southern vegetables: Everything's boiled for nine days in half a gallon of fat—but you'd have to admit the taste is out of this world. And two minutes later so was I.

2

MARY MAC'S

Ponce de Leon used to be a central thoroughfare in Atlanta, now it's just another side street off Peachtree. It leads all the way from one of the hippest old movie houses in the country, the Fox Theatre, to Stone Mountain, the largest piece of exposed granite in the world. And it *is* a big old rock.

Once they tried to tear down the Fox Theatre, but citizen outcry saved it. Once Stone Mountain was surrounded by wild woods, but now it's a genteel citizens' park—admission twenty bucks. That's Atlanta: Tear it down or make money off it, one or the other.

On Ponce we find Mary Mac's Tea Room, purveyor of fine southern cooking for many a year. On a good day it's within walking distance for me. I could fall out of bed on Durant and roll there if I had to. From my joint you've got to head toward the Fox, and away from Easy. That's the club made famous by none other than Dalliance Oglethorpe and her unerring notion of what the citizens will go for. Easy Two is its younger sister in Savannah, where the Saint Patrick's revelry and merriment abound every March.

I don't care much what they say about April in any other place, *March* is fairly cruel in *this* man's town. Just when you think it's spring, around the end of February, and all the buds pop out and the azaleas start to show off, boom comes an ice storm and wrecks the whole agricultural ambience, or what have you. So you're always just a little cautious of everything in March. Looks like spring, but maybe it's not. Could be fine fishing, or could be the big freeze. And aren't the ides of March supposed to be bad news? Whatever the hell an *ide* is. Matters not to me. I'm the cautious type anyway. If it looks like storms *or* ides, I stay inside.

Not sure, but it might have been that I hadn't left the apartment since the day after New Year's. I'm not saying I'm genetically disposed to the shut-in mentality. I just had no particular place to go. Dally was in Savannah. There was nobody else I especially wanted to see, and what with take-out food delivery, I just didn't see the point of getting all agitated and dressed and whatnot. And I had reading to catch up on, after all—although nothing in particular. Still, it was a pretty day at lunchtime on March eighteenth, and a stroll seemed just like what the proverbial doctor might have ordered.

Now, an azalea is a bush from China or some such, but it's done quite well by southern towns. At a certain moment in the spring every single one of them

will conspire to produce red or purple or white flow-
ers that flush out a shrub to no end. And it was along
such a bounteous hedge I wended my way to Mary
Mac's Tea Room. This is to say that my mood was
very bright and gay as they used to say in the old
songs. It was spring. I was out. Food was good. And I
was about to see Dalliance.

She was waiting out front of the place. Too nice a
day to wait inside. She was wearing one of those
spring type of dresses that reminds your head of tu-
lips while the rest of you is caught remembering what
it was like to be a teenager. She saw me coming and
made with the biggest smile possible for a human
face—although mine was by all means giving hers a
run for its money.

"So, big boy—you miss me?"

"Not much." I felt like dancing. "I just haven't
been out of my apartment since you left."

"Well, that was *some* New Year's Eve party.
Would have killed a lesser man."

"Oh, I've still got scars."

"You seem to be healing nicely." She touched my
face.

"Yeah." I nodded. "You look good too, kiddo."

She sighed, like she had more to say, but in the end
it was just, "Let's eat."

Mary Mac's can get right crowded of a lunchtime.
But we were late, the line was short, and we got a
table right away. It was after the big-business types
and luncheon blue hairs had cleared out.

The order tickets were always on the table along
with a slew of pencils, so you made out your own

order. By me there's no beating the chicken livers.
Dally got the country-fried steak, the choice of gour-
mands. Tea so sweet it comes with a side of insulin.
Rolls so good you want to eat the basket they came
in.

I glugled a little tea and took in her countenance.
"You do look good. I guess being an aunt agrees with
you."

"Dutch aunt."

"Uh-huh, but it's quite a drive you're asking me to
do, up to the mountains, and all."

"You suffer from midtowner's disease." She made
a face. "If it's more than a half hour's drive from
home, you don't want to go."

I nodded vigorously. "Absolutely."

"But that means no mountains, no beach, no
farms, no fishing . . ."

"All of which I can watch on the TV, which I got
cable."

"What kind of a life is that?"

I shrugged. "My kind."

"Uh-huh. Are you going to go with me to visit my
kin, or else?"

"That's right, threaten me. That'll make me want
to spend five hours in the car with you."

"It's not five hours."

"Three."

"Okay." She tore a roll. "At least three. But it's a
pretty drive."

"Oxymoron. *Drive* and *pretty* are mutually exclu-
sive."

"Says you. And don't call me a moron."

Luck brought lunch before any more witty retorts could fly. Very fine eats indeed. We were both hungry, and all we talked about for a while there was the food itself.

Then, about coffee-and-bread-pudding time, Dally told me the funny thing about the birth of her new niece.

"On their way to the hospital Mustard and Sissy ran afoul of the Little Girl of Lost Pines."

"The *who*?"

"Usually happens in the early spring like this, or late winter. They saw the ghost."

"Is that right."

She told me the story of Mustard and Sissy's trip to the hospital, complete with the vanishing youngster and the ripping up of some poor schmo's cornfield and all. Belonging, as I do, to the First Church of the Insistent Skeptic, I didn't buy. "It couldn't be that Mustard and Sissy were just tired, it being midnight? Or all wound up from nerves on account of they got a baby arriving? Or maybe they just caught a little red reflector from somebody's mailbox, even?"

She dipped a spoon into my bread pudding. "See, that's your problem. You got no sense of romance."

"Romance?"

"They saw the ghost of the little lost girl, and then they had a baby girl themselves? You don't think it's cool?"

"Not in the least. It's not even lukewarm."

"Must you always play the Doubting Thomas?"

"Must you always regale me with hooey?"

"Hooey?"

"You heard me."

"Listen, buster." She leaned back. "I've got a good mind not to even let you go to the mountains with me this afternoon."

I folded my arms. "Anything but that."

"Everybody in the nation"—she shook her head—"loves a good ghost story."

I raised my eyebrows. "Now I'm *unpatriotic*?"

"Like always."

"Listen, missy, I'm quite fond of a ghost story upon a chilly night beside the campfire, roasting marshmallows and weenies and whatnot. But in general I would rather read a bus schedule than a spook tale."

"Spook tale?"

"I've heard 'em called that."

"In your crowd? I'd imagine you have."

"My crowd? Who's the one always hangs out at *your* bar?"

She knew I had her, so she shifted left. "Come on, Flap, let's go to the mountains."

I gave forth with dismay. "Aw . . . they got no good wine up there, not one drop."

"They got their own *wineries* up there, for chrissake."

"So-called. You know my feelings about American wine."

She looked down slowly. "And you know *my* feelings about this trip."

"You're not going to let me out of it, are you?"

"Not really."

"What's the big deal?" I squinted.

She was a little sterner than I thought she needed to be. "It's important to me. I *have* to go."

"Uh-huh. And you're just going to make me miserable if I don't go with you?"

"As only I can."

"I see." I nodded. "Then I actually have little choice."

She nodded right back. "That's how I see it."

"In that case I'd be delighted."

She smiled sweetly, like the rest of the conversation had never taken place. "I knew you'd come."

3

A GHOST STORY

"So"—I sipped the last of my tea—"where do we get this malarkey about the ghost, anyway?"

"More than fifty years ago"—Dally squinted—"on Black Pine Mountain there lived a happy family and their darling moppet name of Christy."

I slouched down. "I hate it already."

"Christy loved to play at catching fireflies in a jar. She ran around all over the mountain catching them and then letting them go."

"Resulting in all manner of dizzy and confused fireflies."

"One night she ran farther from home than she ever had before, and got lost after dark. She could hear her mother calling, but she could not find her way home."

"Maybe she should've followed the lightning bugs."

"Shut up, they're not like homing pigeons." She

gave me the eye, a look to fry bacon, then returned to her caper. "Far into the night the frantic parents searched and searched, but they never did find their daughter. Grief overtook them, and they died by their own hand, burning down their home in the process."

"Jeez. Nice story."

"Now little Christy is doomed to wander forever, caught betwixt life and death, never to find her own house and family."

"Uh-huh."

"But to this very day, on a moonlit night, in the late-winter wood, more than one resident of the tiny community has seen the little girl, in her bright red dress, catching fireflies at midnight and looking for her long-lost home."

"I've heard enough."

She ignored me. "And that's why they changed the name of the place to Lost Pines."

"And that's where we're going?"

"Lost Pines? Yup."

"I see."

She stood. "And time is, as they say, a-wastin'."

"Where do they say that? Up there? Because if they do, I *really* don't want to go."

She patted my shoulder. "Come on, it'll be fun. You're going to get vistas, an' all."

I played along. "They got actual *vistas* up there in the mountains?"

"Far as the eye can see."

"An' panoramas? How about those?"

She headed toward the door. "Would you just leave the tip? Lunch is on me."

She stopped at the cash register by the door and paid. I dropped a five on the table, which you'd have to say is a fairly heavy tip considering we filled out our own tickets and all. But generosity to wait personnel is a Tucker family trait. We're all quite proud of it.

I caught up with Ms. Oglethorpe. She was nearly out the door. "How long's it been since you saw Sissy?"

She thought for a second. "Gotta be that family reunion with everybody down in Cordele. When was that?"

"Like, last summer. Been almost a year."

I'd gone with her to that reunion. If you play your cards right, and train properly beforehand, you can eat enough food at a family reunion to actually choke a horse. I could go on all day about the corn bread alone. I hadn't seen Dally's relatives in a while myself, and it was kind of like seeing my own kith and kin: a lot of asking me did I have a real job yet, was I ever planning to get married, had I gotten enough to eat— stuff like that.

Dally was close with her cousins on account of her being an only child. And Sissy was like her sister anyway. They looked a little alike, both with the curly auburn hair, the green eyes, and the vaguely patrician demeanor, which is a direct result, they will be happy to tell all and sundry, of being descended from the Oglethorpe who founded Georgia.

James Oglethorpe was a British general and something of a philanthropist. He invented Georgia in 1733 as a refuge for debtors and persecuted Protestants under a special "huddled masses yearning to breathe free" charter. We were a proud colony of wretched refuse from the Mother Country's teeming shore. Today the state's full up with Yankee business types who, most of them, feel they're doing you a *favor* by wrecking everything about the old south in the name of the aforementioned progress of business. Pretty soon there'd be no more *South* left, just *Anyplace USA*, only warmer.

"*What* are you thinking about?"

I realized we were halfway back to my apartment and I'd been absorbed in my lofty mental excursions. "Colonization."

She pointed. "Uh-huh. Look."

It was a pink dogwood just blooming. But the word *pink* doesn't do the color justice. There ought to be a special name just for that color that says a volume and a half about Eastertime and rebirth, warmth and new light.

See, this was one of Dally's many gifts, the ability to bonk me out of a conundrum with a fairly simple wave of the hand. Or, in this case, point of the hand, I guess. If you ever need any soothing of a fevered brain, she's the one to see.

I appreciated the tree, then turned the same appreciative eye her way. "Thanks."

She nodded. She knew. "Also, bud, you get to see Mustard again—on our little sojourn."

I nodded. "Yeah. That'll be swell."

Mustard Abernathy, big as a house, tough as a mile of new highway, was by far the nicest guy in Dally's extended family. He worked his farm,

coached the high school football team, and insisted
that all his players take ballet lessons.

That's right. Mustard and Sissy came into Atlanta
every Christmas to see the Atlanta Ballet do the *Nut-
cracker*, largely because Mustard was fascinated with
the dancers' physical abilities. "How'd they stay up in
the air that long? Look at that guy *lift*! Like it's
nothin'. How do they get those leg muscles?" That
sort of thing.

So he made all his guys take ballet lessons, which
at first embarrassed them to no end. But when they
found out that there were plenty of girls in tights at
the dance classes, things eased up a tad. And when
they discovered that these same girls could kick the
living stuffing out of *any* guy in leg strength, endur-
ance, and general toughness, you couldn't keep the
football team away even with an electric fence and
mad dogs. To make a long story short, as a result of
this somewhat unorthodox practice, Mustard's team
won state every year. It was a source of tremendous
pride for boys who had no money, hard lives, slack
futures, and no way out.

So Mustard was aces with me. Mostly what he
wanted to do in life was help other people. He said it
was on account of his being a Christian, but I've met
so many of them where that's *not* exactly the case
that I had to believe something else was at work.
Whatever. He was just fine by me.

I looked back at the dogwood tree. "Yeah, that'll
be great, seein' Mustard." Then I pointed. "Look,
you got a tree as pretty as this thing, don't you think

you could've come up with a better name than *dog-wood*?"

She smiled. "Well, what's in a name?"

"In this particular one?" I looked back at her. "There's a *dog* in it."

4

VISTAS

Okay, the drive up into the mountains was kind of pretty after all. It was early afternoon and the middle of the week, so there was hardly any traffic. Plus, once you get into the actual mountains, it's some mighty lot of nature going on all over the place. Everywhere there was that new green, the first green. It's like the whole world thought it had just invented the color: "Hey, look at this. We never had this shade before—not exactly *this*."

The air got cleaner, too, and clearer. You could see all the way to Scotland or Ireland if you looked hard enough. That's because most of the people who lived in the Georgia mountains were descended from the Scots and the Irish, who'd settled there to get away from the English in the lowlands. Never been to Scotland, but I'm told the Appalachian hills in Georgia are not unlike the ones they've got over there. I'd like to check it out myself one time—strictly as a matter of research.

Dally was reading the map like it was a good book. "We could take the 575 and go up gradual like, using up a ton of gas, or get on the direct route through the mountain passes and wreck your transmission. Your choice."

"Which takes longer?"

"Oh, now you want to take *longer*?"

"Jeez, Dally, take a gander at this *view*."

She looked up for a second. "'Spretty." Right back to the map. "Could go through Clarksville."

"What's in Clarksville?"

"I don't know."

"So . . ."

She folded the map, nodded her head in the direction of the hood ornament. "Thataway."

Being as it was the only road around, ergo the only way to go, "thataway" was exactly the direction I took.

The mountains got steeper and the air got cooler. There were valley passes like something out of a fantasy movie: "This is the way the world would have been if there had never been men and machines—this is the peace in the valley." There was even snow on the tops of some of the taller peaks. I know lots of people don't think of Georgia as having mountains, and folks from Montana and the like turn their noses up at what they call the Appalachian foothills. But what I was looking at was, as they used to say around the filling station, "a picture no artist could paint." And buddy, they were right.

Now, you come into the bustling community of
Lost Pines before you actually realize there's anything
there. You've got to get up on the actual mountain if
you really want to see where they all *live*. Down on
the main road there's just a couple of stores: Miss
Nina's, aptly named FOOD; and a very retro-looking
gas station that was closed. If you keep going on past
everything toward the big highway past the Wal-
Mart, you get to County General Medical Center, by
far the newest-looking bunch of buildings anywhere
about.

I'm convinced my car made a noise, just as it
turned off, that went something like "Thank God."
Dally didn't hear it, but she was more interested in
getting inside and seeing her new little niece.

The hospital was nice, new, bright—it was a hospital. I don't know what I had expected, maybe
something more town-doctor-living-room-y'all-come.
Anyway I had the same feeling I always had in any
hospital anywhere: the how-soon-can-I-leave feeling.

We sauntered by the picture window where you
can look in at the newborn tykes. They all looked
exactly the same and they all looked very unhappy. I
fancied they had the same hospital feeling I had, and
was taken by a sudden impulse to liberate them all,
take them back down the road to Miss Nina's for
some swell eats. Although I am told a newborn is
nothing but a piker in the food department, and will
only drink milk. Still, I was certain they would have
appreciated the gesture.

Dally spent a lot of time pointing and telling me
how much Baby Girl Abernathy looked like this or

that relative, and I spent a lot of time agreeing. I've found it's often easier just to agree.

When all was said and done, we had decided the nipper looked most like Dalliance Oglethorpe, and trundled off to Sissy's room to tell her so.

The room was a little dark, the curtains being drawn, but Sissy was awake, and nearly blasted out of her blanket when she saw Dally in the doorway. Honest to God, Mustard had to restrain her from getting out of bed.

Dally zoomed into the room and popped a big smack right on Sissy's kisser. It was very heart-warming and what have you, but Mustard and I con-fined our own selves to a handshake.

"Flap."

"Mustard. You got yourselves a cute little wiggler in there."

He grinned. "I reckon we'll keep 'er."

Dally sat on the bed. "Got a name yet?"

Sissy was holding Dally's hand. They really did look like sisters. "Thinkin' about Rose."

Dally approved. "Rose is nice."

I added my two cents. "Long as you don't name it after her daddy, it's all fine by me."

Mustard had to agree. "Girl ought not to be named after a condiment."

But Mustard was joshing, as he was wont to do. In point of fact he had been named after the vegetable mustard greens. When I asked him about it once, he told me that his own mother had given him such a name on account of mustard greens being so easy to plant and to grow—which Mustard had always interpreted as meaning he had been an unplanned bundle of joy.

Dally tried out the new name. "Rose Abernathy. Sounds important."

Mustard nodded. "That's the only thing I don't like about it. Already sounds grown up. She won't have no childish ways about her, name such as that."

Sissy smiled over at the big guy. "You got enough childish ways for the whole entire family unit, mister."

He grinned even bigger. "I believe I do at that." And proud of it.

Then, unexpectedly, Sissy got serious. "Okay, now Dally and Flap's here, you'd best be gettin' on over."

He sighed heavy.

I looked at Dally.

She patted Sissy. "Go *where*, sugar? Something the matter?"

She cast a glance at her husband, who was concentrating his attentions on the very clean hospital floor. It was a silence big enough to park a car in.

Finally he talked sideways at me. "After everything was okay with Sissy an' the baby? I called up over at the McDonner place, tell 'em how it was me that done messed up their side corn land. . . ." but he didn't know how to finish.

She went on for him. "They didn't think nothin' about it, on account of they were out all night looking for their own little girl, Ginny."

Mustard found his voice. "They think she must have got up out of bed an' just wandered off some kind of way."

Sissy helped some more. "Mustard's goin' over to help 'em look."

He looked at me. "You want to go too, bud? They could use a man that's got your peculiar ways about findin' a person."

Sissy got real quiet then. "He needs some company, Flap. We got all kind of questions about this thing." Barely audible. "She was out playin' in her little red jumpsuit at midnight. They say we might be the last ones that seen her."

Mustard nodded at Dally. "I reckon we didn't see no Lost Pines ghost on that highway like I tol' you after all." He looked toward the window, where the light of day was obscured by the dark curtain. "I believe we might have seen the last of Ginny McDonner."

5

MR. SNOW

It was chilly in the woods around sunset, the kind of chill that made you figure winter wasn't quite done yet. Could come up an insult to the entire concept of horticulture: Mr. Snow, the big boss man when the sun's going down. He freezes all the Yankees because he knows they've done wrong. When he comes down south, it's strictly as a visitor. He doesn't move in. Wouldn't do him any good. One mint julep and a smell of magnolia and his whole raison d'être'd get all kerflooey. Still, there was snow in the air.

Mustard and I had been tromping through the woods for about an hour like we knew what we were doing. The leaves were just barely beginning to pop out on the trees, so you could see all through the trees and whatnot. There wasn't a sign of the little kid, not a hint, not a whisper. We hadn't even seen the other searchers since we'd gone down into a small hollow.

Mustard stopped to catch his breath. The big

guy'd been up for nearly twenty-four hours, and it was beginning to show.

"Flap, I got to take a breather, son."

I made with the big halt myself. "I'm entirely hip."

We made quite the pair, I'm guessing. I looked like a fugitive from a Salvation Army thrift store—in my estimation, purveyors of classic haberdashery—and he was strictly pumpkin vine: coveralls, baseball cap, work boots *made* out of mud.

He was pretty grim for an optimist. "She's a goner, Flap. We don' find 'er tonight, she ain't going to make it. I b'lieve it's going to snow."

I tried not looking at him. I thought it would take some of the fatalism out of the idea. Didn't work.

I checked the watch. "Almost six. What time's the sun go down around here?"

"This time of year? 'Round six or so, I reckon."

I looked out at the woods, the long shadows. "Did you know this kid?"

He shook his head. "Naw. I mean, I seen 'er. Cute. They said she was real smart, too."

"How old?"

Shrug. "Ten?"

"And you don't think she'll make it one night out in the woods?"

"Two nights, Flap. This'll be her second one. And if it snows and she don't get in? That little red jump-suit ain't no kind of help from that kind of cold." He shoved himself forward and started walking again. "Doncha find it kind of amazing that just when it looks like spring, it can be winter again?"

I followed after. "I was just thinking the same kind of thing earlier today."

"And ain't it somethin' how the human body don't tolerate?"

"You lost me."

He stepped over a big fallen pine. "Like, if your body temperature goes more than ten degrees—just ten one way or the other? Of what's normal? You can die. Don't seem like much room for variation."

And that right there is one of the many-splendored reasons I was fond of Mustard Abernathy: He was a philosophical type.

We trudged on in silence for a while, watching the shadows stretch out like dark wolves leaning toward dinner, and he was the one to say what we were both thinking. "We better head on back."

Without lights or warmer clothes, we had to start back toward the dirt road where his truck was parked. Still, it felt a whole lot like giving up.

He lowered his voice. "I don't mean nothin' by this, Flap—but why don't you do your trick like you can do and get this little girl back home?"

My trick. I didn't really like to discuss it with anybody. It was doomed to be misunderstood. Dally had blabbed about it at the last family reunion. There's absolutely nothing magical about it, but when you talk about it, I guess it just sounds like I'm pretty squarely off my rocker. It's simple, really: I sit, I dream, and I see the missing pieces. I can find anything in the dream. Then all I've got to do is figure *out* the dream and bingo: success in the material world. It's the thing that gives me an edge in the find-ing-things department. But . . ."

I shook my head. "I can't just close my eyes and make it happen. Doesn't work that way, pal."

"Oh." I could hear him thinking. "How does it work?"

"Like anything else. You've got to wander around, ask questions, gather information, seek for knowl-edge—*then* you can sit down in a nice quiet place and try to stand back while all that junk, like, assembles itself appropriately in your mind's eye or what have you. See, there's nothing hidden, ever. I know every-thing already. Just got to realize it."

He nodded. "*A priori.*"

So blow me down, as they'd say in the funny pa-pers. I had to take a pause on that one. Had to be blunt with the guy: "Huh?"

He shrugged it off. "I watch a lotta that *Nova* on the TV. *A priori* is like prior knowledge—far as I can figure." He sniffed.

How are you *not* in a position to love the guy? "Yeah, well . . . *a priori* knowledge notwithstand-ing, I'm saying you gather all the info, but you don't know what it means until you quit thinking about it. That's the *trick*, to quit thinking about it."

He grinned. "Shoot. I can do that."

"A lotta people think that, but it's harder than you might imagine."

He walked on. "So you got to go, like, talk to the McDonners, other people that knows Ginny, an' all?"

"Right."

"So . . . you actually *are* a detective."

"Keep your voice down. I don't usually like to say the word out loud."

"How come?"

"I don't want anybody getting the idea that I'm a troublemaker—or mistaking me for a guy who knows what he's doing."

We could see the truck. There were a few others pulled off the road close by. We could see a couple of other guys here and there giving up too. Mustard waved. One guy waved back.

He kept his voice down very nicely. "Could you do it anyway? I don't believe I can take the idea of lettin' that little girl go."

Clearly in his voice was the new father, the one who couldn't stand the idea that one day his own little girl might be lost in the woods, and all the men that were out to find her could be walking back toward their trucks on the edge of the wood, silent, failing, cold.

I knew what he meant. I didn't much care for the idea of the kid in the snow myself.

We climbed into the truck. He cranked it up, but he didn't move. At first I thought he was letting it warm up, but I finally realized he was waiting for an answer.

I looked at his profile. "You really think I should do this? You know how some of these people hereabouts take to strangers asking questions. I like this jacket. I'd hate to get buckshot all in it. Makes it very hard to dry-clean."

"I'll go with you."

"And you know everybody."

He nodded. "I do."

"Yeah, well, I still know how naturally unfriendly a place this is."

He shook his head. "Reserved. Not unfriendly."

"Okay."

"Next thing: You got any other kind of clothes?"

I tightened my lips. "Nope. I only got my clothes. I only like my clothes. I only wear my clothes."

He smiled. "Just askin'."

"Uh-huh, and I'm just answering: Lay off the accoutrements."

"Roger that."

"I got my own sense of style."

He agreed. "It's uniquely your own, I'd give you that."

I looked out the window. "Still, I don't much care for the idea of the kid out there in the snow."

He saw the look on my face. "You're going to give it a shot."

I nodded a little. "It's a simple little thing, I guess. Ask a few questions. Find a tyke. If Dally's up for stayin', I'm in."

But there was little doubt that Ms. Oglethorpe would stay. She's the motherly type, in a very strange way. And my own nonchalance was a little deceptive. I was one to take this kind of thing very seriously. If I'm in, I'm in all the way. No half measures. I was going to find Ginny McDonner. I just had no way of knowing how wrong I was about it's being a simple little thing.

6

MISS NINA

By seven-thirty Dally, Mustard, and I had eaten. Miss Nina's FOOD was superb dining; the woman was a rural epicure. There were no employees, only the owner herself, and she was well into her sixties. She arose at five every morning and started setting pots on the three stovetops in the backroom. By noon everything had been boiled or fried to her satisfaction, and she'd open the doors to the front room, which might have been a drugstore or a feed store at some time in the past. There were maybe twenty tables and a soda-fountain-type bar.

By one-thirty in the afternoon Miss Nina always went home, upstairs, for a nap. But she was back at five for the dinner crowd, and she closed at seven. We'd made it just in time. Miss Nina was barely awake in a rocker by the heat-stove in the outer room. We handed her our three bucks, following Mustard's lead as he wandered into the kitchen.

Stacked up on a table were the plates and napkins. In a shoebox beside them were the eating utensils. All a customer needed to do was heap creamed corn and country-fried steak and black-eyed peas and collards and fried chicken and boiled green beans on a plate— and then try to get to a table without spilling any.

The tables were set with jars of iced tea and a big wad of foil that was supposed to have kept the corn-bread warm. There was no talk, not in the whole place. By seven-thirty we three were the last ones in the joint. Miss Nina'd shuffled upstairs just after she'd locked the doors and told Mustard to make sure it closed real tight and locked when we left.

He was staring into his glass of tea. "Okay, bud— where do we start?"

I turned to Dally. "Something of a coincidence, this little story of the little girl of Lost Pines in conjunction with the currently missing Ginny McDonner."

She nodded. "And I know how you feel about co-incidence."

Mustard looked at her—it was a question.

She answered. "He doesn't believe in 'em."

"They *always* mean something." I smiled at him. "Always."

He set his glass down. "Well, in point of fact I believe I'm the one that brought it up."

I leaned my elbows on the table. "So, what's the *real* story?"

He shook his head. "Whatchu mean?"

"I mean there's more to the story. There always is.

What I heard was the folktale. I want the tabloid version."

Mustard looked away. "Well . . . Daddy did tell me somethin' once. He didn't like to bring it up. I was about twelve, I remember, and I told him I's a'run away like that old Christy girl. I reckon I was mad about somethin' or another. I could tell right away Daddy's troubled in his head. He said, 'You don' want to be like that, boy.' And this is what he tol' me was the *real* story."

He settled back. "That little girl's daddy was *significantly* the best corn-liquor man in this county. Made the best corn liquor you ever tasted. So clear it was invisible in the jar. So pure it healed the sick at heart and made the lame to walk. Also made the walkin' lame—if they had too much."

Dally understood. "He was an artist."

Mustard stuck out his lower lip. "I've heard it said that a'way."

I encouraged. "And . . ."

Mustard's face tightened. "And one night"—he looked at his tea again—"maybe more than one night, but this one night in particular . . . he was drunk and took out after his own little girl but good."

Dally squinted. "Like how?"

He nodded. "Like, with a belt, they say—wailed the tar out of 'er. She brought in a jar of fireflies, inside the house to show 'im? He got mad on account of it was one of his liquor jars. He didn't want her messin' with his things. They say he busted the jar on her head and then took a belt to her so bad, she run out the house screamin' so loud everybody on the mountain heard it. She run into the woods, to a hidin' place she had: little ol' tree hut made out of pine straw. When I was a kid, they used to tell me it was still out there somewheres."

I raised my eyebrows. "Well, this is a *much* worse story than I'd like to hear right now."

He nodded. "Uh-huh. And when they couldn't find her, the mama threatened to leave the daddy, and they was a big fight. And then the ol' boy got more an' more drunk and worked his still too much, and they say it blowed up."

Dally nodded. "That's the fire that burned down the house?"

He shrugged. "They say."

I shoved my dinner plate away from me. "So what really happened to the little girl?"

He looked at me, finally. "Oh, they never did find her." He lowered his voice. "I don't want you'uns to think I'm out my mind—but I seen her before last night. I don't mean like just a blink or a scratch. I've seen 'er walking in these woods. Lots of folks up here have. It's a dark night on a back road or out night fishin' . . ."

I rubbed my eyes. I guess I was tired. "Yeah. Okay."

Dally leaned over to Mustard. "Any of that family still around?"

He raised his eyebrows. "I don' know."

I closed my eyes. "Well . . . I guess, in answer to your earlier question, we start talking to people. Somebody might have seen something."

Mustard didn't seem enthusiastic. "They woulda said . . ."

But Dally moved like she was about to get up. "They might have seen something only they didn't *know* it." And she fluttered her eyes in my direction.

FOLK ART

By eight o'clock we were all standing on the Wicher front porch, at the next house over from the McDonners'. Mr. Wicher was holding the door nearly closed and leaning on the inside frame.

"Mustard?"

But he was looking at Dally and me.

Mustard cleared his throat. "This here's Ms. Oglethorpe, Sissy's cousin from Atlanta. She come up to see the baby."

He nodded. "Heard you had it."

Mustard acknowledged. "Did."

Dally tried valiantly. "Hey."

Mr. Wicher barely nodded, staring at me.

Mustard went on with the introductions. "An' that's Flap Tucker. He's goin' to find Ginny McDonner."

"Oh, he is." Mr. Wicher, it seemed, was also something of a Doubting Thomas—although I am by no means implying that we were on a first-name basis.

Mustard nodded. "Yup. Needs to ask you a few things."

Mr. Wicher pushed back from the doorframe, away from us. "Don't know nothin' about it." And he was on the verge of closing the door without any further niceties.

I saved the day. "Oh, you'd be surprised. A lot of people who feel like they don't know anything at all turn out to be quite bright about a subject, once you get in out of the cold and maybe a cup of coffee—get to know 'em and all."

He scrolled his eye at me, obviously angry for no good reason. "What?"

I was fearless. "I said maybe you know more about this than you realize." Big smile.

He opened the door and took a step toward me. "Looka here. I got no use for you. I got little use for Abernathy. I don't give a damn if you freeze to death out here. This is my property, an' I'm tellin' you three to clear out, *right* now! Get off my porch. Get off my land."

Dally scooted back; Mustard stood his ground, looking at me; and I shot out my right hand like it was a twenty-dollar bill I was giving away. "Listen, brother, I've got nothing in mind but finding that little girl before the temperature drops any lower. Now . . . why wouldn't you want to help us with a thing like *that* . . . if you could?"

He didn't take my hand, but quite unexpectedly he

stopped. He sniffed. He softened. "They do say it might snow tonight."

Mustard nodded, looking down at the porch floor. "I believe it might."

Mr. Wicher looked at Dally, took in a long, deep breath and sighed it out. "Would you like to come in the house, ma'am? Maybe have a cup of coffee? It's kindly cold out here on this porch, ain't it?"

She smiled. "Uh-huh."

He shoved the door back and turned away from us.

Dally went in first, whispering to me, "Nice work, kiddo. Coulda got us shot."

Mustard disagreed. "Naw . . . Wicher might cut you, but he ain't got no good kind of gun in the house."

I let him go before me too. "Does he greet all his visitors like this?"

Mustard smiled and nodded.

Wicher had vanished. We followed Mustard into the sitting room. There was a very hot cast-iron stove at an outside wall—the only light in the room—and a big knife right in the middle of the floor.

Mustard grinned at me and pointed at the knife. "See."

Dally was a little less bon vivant. "What's *that* there for?"

Wicher appeared, suddenly, out of the shadows. "Carvin'."

We all jumped just a little.

He ignored us; sat in the chair closest to the knife.

"Coffee's on." He made no indication whatsoever of where he wanted the rest of us to take a load off.

Dally slipped into the chair farthest away from our host, leaving Mustard and me to slap down side by side on the sofa.

She was still bold. "Carving?"

He nodded, leaned over to pick up the knife. I leaned forward just a little, but out of the corner of my eye I could see Mustard shake his head.

Wicher picked up a foot-long hunk of wood he'd apparently been working on when we'd come to the door. It was shaped kind of like a giant clothespin. It came out of a pile of stuff on the dark side of the chair, where something else caught my eye.

He held it up. "See?"

Dally nodded. She had no idea what she was looking at. "Nice."

He looked at it. "Going to be blue."

Dally smiled a little. "I like blue."

Mustard agreed. "It's a nice color."

But me? I'm a dope. I had to know. "What is it?"

Wicher cocked his head at it. "Once I get the arms on it, stick half a clothes hanger through it, and counterweight it with a big old wooden bass, it'll be a fisherman. Balances on the edge of things—things like a table an' all. You can rock it back and forth, and it won't fall over, if I get it right."

Mustard put the final touches on the explanation. "Folk art. It's a big seller come summer when all the northsiders run up here from Atlanta."

He agreed. "Them an' the rotor-ducks."

Dally's turn for curiosity. "Rotor-ducks?"

He nodded at her. " 'Swhat I call 'em."

Once again, Mustard toured us through the world of primitive sculpture. "It's a duck that's got, like, propellers for wings, so that when the wind blows, they run around an' 'round. Looks nice."

Wicher set his knife down. "Usually paint *them* things red."

Dally relaxed a little. "Is that what you do?"

"Do?"

"I mean for a living . . ."

He actually smiled. "Shoot."

Mustard clued us in as to the sudden outburst of levity. "He's got his own farm here. Does pretty good, don't it?"

He gave a single nod, set down his wooden fisherman. "That carvin' an all, that's just what I do of an evenin'—so the time'll go by. I do a little carpentry from time to time, cabinetmakin' and such as that . . ."

I sat forward. "Well, we won't take up much more of your evening. I was just wanting to ask you a few things."

He stood up. "Coffee's ready." And he left.

Mustard stood up too. "We can go in the kitchen now."

We followed again. The kitchen was much brighter and there were four mugs set around the kitchen table. Mustard waited until our host had poured the coffee and taken a seat, and then he sat down. We followed suit.

Loath as I was to waste more time: "Did you know Ginny McDonner?"

"Seen her."

"She ever come over here?"

He nodded, not looking at me. "She likes to watch the ducks."

"The wooden ducks."

"Uh-huh."

I took a sip. "When's the last time you saw her?"

"Last night."

"Really. Where?"

"In the road."

Dally set her mug down. "In the middle of the road?" She looked at Mustard.

He nodded. "I believe we did too—takin' Sissy to the hospital."

I tried to get Wicher to look me in the eye. No dice. I leaned back. "About what time did you see her, Mr. Wicher?"

Shrug. "Ten?"

I looked at Mustard. "You didn't see her till after midnight."

He nodded.

Dally shifted in her seat. "Well, she wasn't playing out in the middle of the road for two hours."

I looked down at the table. "What was she wearing?"

Wicher squinted. "Red." He sipped. "Could have been midnight."

"How'd you happen to see her?"

"I was out on the porch, carvin'."

I sipped again. "Isn't midnight a little *late* for folks up here?"

"I don't sleep that well." He looked away.

"Maybe you drink too much coffee at night." I couldn't help it. "Is there a Mrs. Wicher?"

Still looking over at the general area of the percolator, he took in a long breath. "I used to be married."

Mustard lowered his voice. "She's passed on."

"Sorry." I looked at my cup. "Any kids?"

Mustard looked at me. "She died birthin' their first."

"Baby died too." Wicher's voice was hollow.

Dally finished her coffee. "I think we're about finished with this particular subject."

I disagreed. "Mr. Wicher . . . how often did Ginny come over here?"

"Well . . ." His eyes drifted back in my general direction. "Near ever' day."

"Really. How come?"

"I make . . . little toys for 'er."

"I thought I saw something like that out in the sitting room." That's what I'd seen in the pile on the dark side of his chair that had caught my eye: dolls.

"It's a little wooden family." His voice was soft. "I been makin' 'em for a while. I built her a dollhouse too. Plays with it all the time."

Dally got caught up in my line of thinking. "Where's the dollhouse, here or at her home?"

He took a long sip of coffee. "Here."

I think I surprised both my cohorts by finishing my coffee and shoving back from the table. "Okay. Thanks."

Mustard squinted. "You *done*?"

I stood. "It's late. It's cold. I want to cover as

much territory as I can. You've got me thinking about the kid out there in the woods and I have a kind of a sense of urgency about the matter."

Dally didn't know what was going on, but she went along anyway. "Mr. Wicher, thanks for the coffee."

He nodded. "Ma'am."

Mustard looked at us both, then down at Wicher. "You want to come out tomorrow an' help us look some more?"

He didn't stand. "Might."

Mustard stood up too and headed for the front door. "Okay. I'll be by early."

He didn't see us out.

Then, just as we were closing the front door, the strangest thing happened. We all heard him speaking very clearly, even though it was obvious he wasn't talking to us.

His voice was hushed. "Well, what do you make of that?"

Pause.

"I know, but they've got to know everything. Don't you want them to find her?"

Pause.

"Sorry. I know you do. I must be gettin' a little tired. You ready for bed?"

That was all we heard.

Dally waited until we were in Mustard's truck to ask, "What was *that*?"

Mustard cranked up the engine. "He was talkin' to his dead wife. He believes her spirit is still in the house."

Dally leaned forward. "He's nuts?"

Mustard smiled. "Naw. He's just lonesome."

Dally shook her head. "Yeah, but . . . he *talks* to her."

Mustard twisted around to see backing the truck out. "Well . . . I seen *her* too."

I had to butt in. "What? You got too vivid an imagination, pal."

He nodded. "I seen her. Once on the stairs, and once or twice out in the field."

Dally wouldn't have it. "Mustard . . ."

He was calm. "Everybody knows how he talks to her. Makes him feel better. And it's a powerful belief. You be around 'im long enough, you believe she's there too."

The headlights of the truck cut out across the sightless black of the night, down the long road where Ginny McDonner had gone. Just as we pulled onto it, the snow began to fall.

8

GUILT

We drove for a while in silence before Dally nearly busted. "What the *hell* did we leave then for? Things were just heating up. That guy's *nuts*."

Mustard chimed in. "I was kind of wonderin' about that myself."

I was staring at the little strikes of snow. You could only see them in the headlights. I tried for the disingenuous. "You think he's got something to do with Ginny McDonner's disappearance?"

Dally shifted uncomfortably in between Mustard and me in the big old front seat of his truck. "Well, you've got to admit . . ." But upon reflection, she did not, as it turned out, know exactly *what* you had to admit.

I nodded. "He's a lonely old guy."

Mustard agreed. "He don' mean nothin' by all that . . . talkin' to his dead wife an' all." He turned on his windshield wipers. "He's all right."

Dally didn't want to let it go. "The guy practically tells us he's the last one to see the kid, and he dotes on her in something of an unhealthy fashion . . ."

I nodded. ". . . the psychology of which is entirely understandable, what with his wife and baby dead and gone."

She folded her arms. "Uh-huh. Plus, a guy sees a little kid playin' in the middle of the road at midnight and he just sits there on his porch?"

Mustard spoke low. "We all try to mind our own business around here."

I tapped Dally on the forearm. "Actually, I'm with you on the last point. The guy dotes on her in the aforementioned psychological fashion, how come he doesn't say 'Get out of the road' or some such?" I looked back out at the snow. "Not to mention how come she was out there in the first place?"

Mustard caught on right away. "So I guess we ought to go talk to the actual parents of the child. They next down the road."

Dally was nodding her head, thinking. "What was she doing out there that *late*?"

Mustard turned into a dirt drive not far down from Wicher's and on the other side of the main road. There was only one light on at the McDonner place, upstairs. It was a farmhouse like a lot of others around, two stories, big wraparound porch with a swing—far as I could tell it was painted white.

Mustard pulled up nearly to the porch, turned off the engine, left the lights on, and just sat there.

Dally looked at him. "Well?"

He just stared at the upstairs window, where, I

assumed, the McDonners were. Sure enough, after a moment or two the window opened and some old guy shoved his head out.

"Who's that in the yard?"

Mustard rolled down his window. "It's Mustard Abernathy, Mr. McDonner. Sorry to bother—I know ever'body been up all night an' day, but some of them boys told us you'uns came on home to change clothes and get some coffee before you went back out—and this is kindly important."

Mr. McDonner craned his neck. "Who's with you?"

"It's Sissy's cousin Dally from Atlanta, an' her friend Flap Tucker. He's the man that's goin' to find Ginny."

Silence. Then a voice in the room with him. Didn't hear what she said.

He waved. "Be down directly." He didn't sound happy.

The window slammed shut. When the lights came on on the porch, Mustard turned off his headlights and we all piled out of the truck. The McDonners were there at the door to greet us.

She was shy and quiet. He was at least fifteen years her senior. Not exactly what you'd ever mistake for exuberant, but a little friendlier than Wicher.

He shook every hand, but his greeting was only slightly less hostile than Wicher's. "Come on in the house. This here's the wife, Maggie."

She nodded and looked down.

We all went right into the kitchen, something of a breech of country protocol, I gathered.

The mister looked at my shoes. "So you're goin' to find my little girl, are you?"

I knew what he wanted to hear. "Yes I am." Simple as that.

Dally made assurances. "He doesn't often say that."

McDonner sat at the kitchen table. "When *does* he say that?" Dripping doubt.

Dally smiled back sweetly. "When he means it. It's a promise."

Mrs. McDonner, right away accepting all my locational prowess, went straight to the heart of the matter. "Will she still be alive?"

I took my seat at the table across from Mr. McDonner; remained mute.

Mustard saved the day. "We just got to ask you both a few little questions, then we be on our way."

Mrs. McDonner was already fixing coffee. She looked in the icebox. "You'uns want some pie?"

Her husband tried to smile. "Chocolate. Ginny's favorite."

Mrs. McDonner started to cry, but she turned away.

Mustard took his seat. "I could eat me a piece."

Mr. McDonner looked at me. "The wife made it herself—it ain't no store pie."

"Then I'd better have some." I smiled back at him, tried to ignore the gloom.

Dally was caught. She knew she was supposed to refuse pie and help serve, she was brought up in the rural South long enough to know what the rules were. But it just wasn't remotely her world. She didn't want to offend, but she didn't want to play the game.

I looked at her. "Would you mind sharing my piece? I'm kind of full from Miss Nina's."

McDonner went right on, obviously trying for some sort of bizarre mountain take on the bon vivant. "Hear that's some good eatin' over there." Then he looked at his wife, who was still sniffling, and his face clouded over again. "We never been."

Dally slipped into a seat beside me. "I think I can help you out, big boy." Nice smile. "Thanks."

Mustard patted at me, working to lighten the Gothic atmosphere in the room. "He *is* going to be a big boy he keeps eatin' like he done today."

I gave him the eye. "Look who's talking."

Mr. McDonner knew we were avoiding the issue. He was tired and worried and I could see he was the kind of a guy that would never show me what he was thinking or feeling. He was a true-blue mountain-ite, or whatever you'd call it. That face would be a mask until the day he died. There in the kitchen, he just wanted to get on with it. "What you need to ask me?"

Dally popped the first question. "What was Ginny doing up so late the other night? Wicher next door saw her—and Mustard saw her a little after midnight—out on the main road."

He looked over at his wife. She stopped what she was doing, still looking away from us to hide her tears.

Mustard urged them on. "I *did* see her."

Mrs. McDonner answered, barely above a whisper. "She sleepwalks."

Her husband nodded and made as to explain. "Walks in her sleep."

She went on. "I usually wake up when I hear her get out of the bed, but that night I reckon I was just wore out. Didn't hear nothin' . . ."

He helped her out. "Ginny's so quiet when she gets up."

She went back to work fixing the coffee. "We didn't even know she was gone till we woke up on account of hearin' Abernathy's truck in our yard."

I nodded. "What time you all usually get up?"

He leaned forward, not looking at anything, very weary. "I usually try to be up by five this time of year."

She wasn't looking our way. "There's so much to do."

Mustard looked over to us. "Gettin' the ground ready to plant, an' all."

McDonner nodded slowly. "It's a lot to do."

I looked at the tabletop. Nice old-timey Formica pattern. Reminded me of my great-grandmother's farm. "So when Mustard called you all this morning . . ."

He understood. ". . . We'd already been up for a couple hours. Seen what happened to the corn patch. We thought it might had somethin' to do with Ginny's . . . bein' gone."

I shook my head. "How do you mean?"

He shrugged. "Sudden noise, got into 'er. Got her scared. I don' know . . ."

She still didn't look our way. "It really scared *us*."

Mustard looked down. "Sorry."

Mrs. McDonner smiled at him, wiped her face a little. "She walks in her sleep no matter what. You didn't do nothin'." Very kindly.

Dally piped up. "Now . . . if you're just now getting ready to plant, how did Mustard ruin your corn patch?"

They all looked at her.

Mustard answered. "I didn't explain that very good. It's where they always do corn. It's got the stalks and all stacked up in it—to plow under. He had it all set to do, an' I messed it up. Tore up the dirt good, too, I reckon."

Mr. McDonner shrugged. "It ain't so bad."

Dally looked at him. "But there's no actual corn there now."

McDonner shook his head. "Naw. You see outside right this minute why we don' plant nothin' this early. March. It's liable to come up a snow or a ice storm."

Dally, mostly to prove she really *did* understand this stuff, asserted her own agricultural prowess. "So you don't plant until after Easter."

Nods all around.

I cleared my throat. "Well . . . glad we got that straight, but what about Ginny?"

Mrs. McDonner looked at me, setting down a cup of coffee in front of Dally. "What about her?"

"Has she ever run off like this before—for instance?"

Both parents looked down. It was like a synchronized swimming event. Dally flashed me a gander. Once again I understood the mountain way: They'd *never* tell us everything. And they were *proud* of their ability to keep grief to a minimum.

I didn't wait for verbal confirmation of my suspicions. Just went right on with the questions. "When was the last time?"

Ginny's mother sighed in what I felt to be a significantly hefty manner, but made no other answer.

Mr. McDonner was left to explain in a very quiet voice. "Happens all the time, really. We just usually hear it, is all. Catch 'er before she's out the house."

Mustard was genuinely curious. "Whatchu reckon causes a little girl to walk in her sleep?"

Mrs. McDonner spoke like it was being ripped out of her. "Doctor says it'll pass." She looked at me. "She's a real . . . *active* li'l thing."

Himself nodded. "Don't *never* want to sit still in the church."

Mustard nodded sagely. "Wiggle-itis."

So dumb it handed us all a laugh—which was the big boy's intention. It was a good thing. Mrs. McDonner finished her coffee and pie service, patted Mustard on the shoulder. "You're a mess."

He went on. "Ain't nothin' to bein' a doctor. All is you got to do is add a 'itis' to near 'bout anything. That's what they call a diagnosis."

Appreciative of the levity as I was, I pressed on. "So what happens? She usually wake up back in bed, or you have to wake her up, or what?"

Dally leaned in. "Always heard you weren't supposed to wake up a sleepwalker."

Mother shrugged. "Don't seem to matter. Sometimes we call out her name and she just snaps right out of it. Sometimes it's like she's in a dreamland."

I kept at it. "Take any medication?"

"Ginny? Naw."

I caught it. "Do *you*?"

She nodded. "Can't sleep sometimes. Doctor says it's worry."

But I could see her husband give her a look, and I could tell she was suddenly sorry she'd told me.

I looked back at the tabletop. "Take any last night?"

Her voice was far away. "Oh. I . . ."

Mr. McDonner was starting to get a little miffed with me, or what have you. "She needs her rest."

I nodded heartily. "Right."

He charged right ahead. "I didn't hear Ginny get up neither, an' I didn't take no medicine."

Mustard stepped in. "He don't mean nothin' by it, Mr. McDonner. He just needs to know ever'thing. Tha's how he works."

Mr. McDonner was a little agitated by now. "Well, I don't b'lieve I much *care* for how he works."

See, that's your human psychology for you: If you feel guilty about something—or terrible about something—all it takes is for somebody to *mention* it, and you end up feeling *accused*. I like to think I'm a kind of a student of that sort of thing. When people snarl at you, it's usually because they've got something of their *own* stuck in some craw or another. At least that's how I think Freud used to explain it.

I spoke very softly. "All I want to do is find Ginny

as soon as possible. That's all that's on my mind." I slipped him a shot of sincerity. "No kidding."

He reassessed. He breathed out. "Right. Sorry. I know that. I'm just . . . all . . ."

I shook my head. "Me too."

Dally filled in. "We're all worried."

And I thought the missus might take up crying again at that. "You don't know what a comfort it is to have you say that."

Clearly these were people who were not in the custom of asking for help, certainly not in the habit of expecting it. And they certainly didn't seem like people that had ever had to count on the county police before. We were apparently something of a surprise.

I couldn't stop now, though. "We talked to Wicher. He saw her."

They both tried not to look at anything. It was kind of amazing, the way they were just staring into space. Finally the mister took a whack at answering me. "We done told her not to go over there again."

His wife, still in shallow voice: "That Mr. Wicher is an odd'n."

Mr. McDonner nodded. "He makes her these little toys an' such . . ."

Dally stuck out her lip. "We saw 'em."

Mustard shrugged. "I thought they were nice."

Mr. McDonner shot him a look. "He needs to keep away from my little girl."

Mustard smiled. "He don't mean nothin' by it."

Ginny's mother disagreed. "He keeps her there after we tell her to come on home"—drop in volume—"an' he calls her by a different name."

Dally got there first. "A different name?"

She was barely audible. "He don't call her Ginny . . ." A whisper: "He calls her *Christy*."

I thought I was being cagey. "That's what he was going to name his own little girl."

But Mustard shook his big old head. "Nope. Christy . . . that there is the name of the little lost girl."

I sat back. "From the spook tale?" I squinted. "That's right, I think Ms. Oglethorpe told me her name was Christy."

He only lifted one shoulder this time. "Tha's what her name was."

"You're right." Dally looked at Mrs. McDonner. "That's too creepy."

She nodded back. "Uh-huh."

"Uh, look—" I wanted to slide right over that little chunk of information, "Mustard said y'all have plenty of relatives hereabout. They're all out looking for the little girl?"

Mr. McDonner tilted his head in his wife's direction. "Friend of her brother's a policeman. That's who's headed up the search."

I looked at him. "The policeman?"

He nodded.

I smiled at his wife. "What's his name?"

"Cedar."

"Like the tree?"

She shook her head. "Short for Cedric."

I was too tired to point out that both names had in fact the same number of syllables. "Last name?"

"Duffie."

"Okay. What about other relatives, like people Ginny might try to get to if she's out wandering?"

Mr. McDonner thought about it. "She likes our preacher. She goes over there a good bit."

"His name?"

"David."

"Last name."

They looked at each other. She answered. "Don't know. He's just David."

"He come over hereabout"—Mustard looked at the grieving parents—"what? Near twenty years ago?"

The mister nodded. "I reckon about that."

Mustard continued. "Said he come down from North Ca'lina. Used to be a ol' drunk. Now he's a preacher. Good'n too."

Mrs. McDonner had a touch of actual awe in her voice. "He's the finest man I ever knew."

Even Mr. McDonner, whom I assessed as something of a skeptic, nodded with a kind of abstract fervency.

I looked at them. "I'd like to meet him."

"Can do." Mustard nodded once, then finished his pie.

I likewise finished my coffee. Dally'd already taken care of the pie. "So, sorry to ask, Ms. McDonner, but when did you start taking the pills?"

"Good while back." Then she shot a glance at the husband.

"What for," I pressed, "do you mind my asking?"

He answered. "Nerves."

I kept my eye on her. "What are you nervous about?"

He still answered. "Been that a'way all her life."

"Really?" I wouldn't let go.

She broke eye contact, examined the Formica herself. "Got the prescription a year after Ginny's born."

Mr. McDonner could barely contain himself. "That's enough." Louder. "I believe we can do without all this." Still louder. "My wife needs her sleep." He stood.

And that, I had to assume, would conclude our broadcast day. Dally stood too, quickly. She shot out her hand to Mr. McDonner. "You're absolutely right. We've taken up enough of your time in the middle of the night. You've got other things to do. We'll be going."

Mustard heaved himself up from his chair. "We check back in the mornin', okay?"

The man of the house nodded curtly.

I was the last to my feet. I locked eyes with the guy. "I'm *going* to find your daughter." Even to me it sounded more like a threat than a promise, and I had no idea why it came out that way.

Dally noticed it right away; shot me a look that could scour a battleship.

But Mrs. McDonner, bless her, looked up at me, her eyes an unashamed variation of red. "Thank you, Mr. Tucker." Softer. "Ginny's the most precious thing there is in this life."

The look on her face had me convinced—Ginny was exactly that important.

HOLY WITH VISION

We said our good-byes and got out to the truck in record time. It was really getting chilly. The snow was thicker. You could see it without benefit of head-lights.

Dally pounded the dash. "Get this heat on, Mus-tard."

He shifted into second and swung the truck around in the yard. "Take it a second to get hot, girl."

She wasn't consoled. "I'm freezing."

"It's not just the weather, you know." I looked out the window. "You're stuck as much by the ice of the situation as you are by the cold in the air."

She wouldn't hear of it. "Is that right, Dr. Freud?"

"Funny you should mention, I was just thinking of the good doctor inside just now."

She was still edgy. "Oh?"

I was unwilling to give over to her mood. "Yes, *oh.*

I was thinking, among other things, about the exact nature of a ghost."

That got her. She quit fidgeting. "A *what*?"

Mustard was helpful. "He said *a ghost*."

I pressed on. "Oh, I know there's some that'll try an' tell you it's got something to do with ectoplasm and spiritual residue and whatnot, but I know better. A ghost is in the eye of the beholder. A ghost is the manifestation of the beholder's guilt."

She was willing to play. "Say, you have been Freudenizing."

"Yes, I have. And you can toss in Jung, too, 'cause I got an explanation for the Little Girl of Lost Mountain, or whatever you call her."

She settled back. "I can't *wait* to hear this."

"Did you know that every year the ghost of Anne Boleyn haunts Blickling Hall, the place of her birth—every May nineteenth, on her birthday. She's seen sitting in a coach carrying her own head on her knee."

Dally's exaggerated diction passed quite well for sarcasm. "Seen . . . by *whom*?"

"*Aha!*" I had her. "That's just the deal. *Everybody* sees it."

She let go of the attitude. "I'm not following this."

"It's your Jungian Universal Unconscious. Everybody that sees her ghost shares in the collective guilt of a country that would chop off a poor girl's head just because she had a daughter instead of a son."

"They chopped her head off because she had Elizabeth. I read a little, too, you know."

I folded my arms. "That's right. Henry the Eighth wanted to have a son. Anne had a daughter, who got to be Queen Elizabeth, by the way. But Henry didn't care about that, he just wanted a son. He said it was her fault that they'd spawned a girl-child, so he lopped off her crown."

"Jeez. And you think—"

"The collective unconscious of England is so guilty over the deal, they actually see her ghost."

Mustard piped up. "An' you think that all us around here see the Little Lost Girl because we got guilt about *her*?"

I tapped Dally on the arm. "See. Mr. Abernathy understands me."

He kept his eyes glued to the road. "No, I don't. What do I got to have any guilt feelin's about that poor little girl?"

I shook my head. "Not you personally. It's the whole town. There's a palpable kind of depressive psychological energy around here that feels it ought *not* to have let a thing like that happen."

Dally looked at me sideways. "What in the *hell* have you been reading?" She leaned forward, rife with mock concern. "Oh my God, it's more of that damn Joseph Campbell, isn't it?"

I nodded, hedging. "It's good. It puts me to sleep at night."

"I'll bet. But just whose guilt are we talking about?"

"The McDonners' . . . to start with. They're pretty jumpy about that medication—the little girl's sleepwalking condition, *and* their funny little neighbor. . . . I'm saying they've got something to hide."

Dally looked at Mustard. "Know if they have any family skeletons?"

He shook his head. "Not as I know of."

I looked at him. "Worth finding out."

But Mustard brought us back to the immediate. "I'm headed over to Cedar's house. I guess that's where we want to go."

I shifted. "Uh. Oh. Yeah." I put my hands up close to the heat vent. "You know him?"

"Sure do. He's a good ol' fella."

Dally tucked her hands under her arms. "Andy or Barney?"

I knew what she was asking. The common joke about small-town cops was that they fell into one of two categories. One was a genuine guy who really cared about the right thing and how to do it. The other was a harmless incompetent with a fair measure of foolish pretension.

Mustard shook off the stereotypes. "I don't like to joke around about Cedar Duffie. He's prob'ly the finest policeman in the United States."

Dally shoved an elbow at him. "This is an uncharacteristic bit of reverence."

He nodded in a fairly solemn fashion. "I'm not kiddin'. He was a *Marine*. He's the real thing. He come back here after seein' the world on account of he thought he could help us up here. I admire the man."

Dally nodded. "I gathered."

I switched the subject. "So you noticed how jumpy everybody at the McDonner household was about medication."

Dally leaned my way. "Well—yeah." It was obvious.

"Wonder what she takes it for."

Mustard shook his head. "I don' know—but she *did* change, like, in her personality—about a year after Ginny was born. She used to be out an' about all the time. Now she'll spend the most of her time workin' around the place . . . or over there at the church."

That was worth noting. I remembered the look in her eye when she was talking about Preacher Dave. I took a stare out the side window. "What kind of church is it?"

Mustard did not make fun. "They take up snakes."

I couldn't see it happen, but I knew Dally was rolling her eyes. "Snake handlers?"

Mustard nodded. "It's a real thing, hon. They drink lye too."

That was a new one. I knew about snake handling, but, "Lye?"

He was very matter-of-fact. "Or some kind of poison. Drink it right down. Don't bother 'em a bit."

I had to know. "Speaking of 'bit'—the snakes ever get anybody?"

He shook his head. "Naw. It's really somethin'."

Foolishly Dally looked to me for the answer. "What's the idea there, exactly?"

And as fate would have it, I felt I had the educational wherewithal to mouth off. "Bible says, 'And they shall take up serpents'—but the serpents won't harm you if you have the Holy Spirit on you."

Her turn to shake her head. "Only in America."

But I had to set her straight. "Well . . . actually no."

"What do you mean?"

"And I quote: 'Allowing Tao to come into you makes you innocent like a child—whom poisonous serpents will not bite, wild animals attack, nor birds of prey approach.' So how do you like *that*?"

Mustard leaned his ear my way. "What's that from, that quote?"

Dally answered for me. "Tao Te Ching—another book that puts our boy here to sleep at night."

"What is it, Chinese?"

She shrugged. "I guess."

He cocked his head. "Is it old? I mean, like, old as the Bible?"

I nodded. "Some say older."

He smiled. "Huh?"

Dally looked at me, and the edge was off. "You never cease to amaze me."

I looked at her, that plum of a kisser. "Yeah, well, if I ever do—let me know, will you? I'd like to do something about it."

She settled in just a little closer to me. "Will do."

We plowed through the accumulating snow, skidded a little into the next driveway. It was the smallest house yet, and an all-brick job. There was a four-wheel-drive jeep of some sort parked in the front. Had cop lights on top.

Before we had even pulled up to the house, the porch light was on.

In the doorway there stood a rock of a man.

Looked a little like a young Victor Mature with a crew cut. His clothes were messy and torn, like he'd spent most of the day crawling through the woods. He looked exhausted.

He held his hand up against the glare of the headlights. "That you, Abernathy?"

Mustard called out. "Yup. Got some visitors, too, bud."

He was craning his neck to see us. "Who are they?"

Mustard cranked off the engine. "It's Sissy's cousin Dally an' her friend Flap Tucker."

He squinted, his eyes adjusting. "Flap Tucker? From Atlanta?"

Dally eyed me. "Your reputation precedes you. What, didja leave a girlfriend up here?"

Mustard tried to help me out, looked at Cedar. "You *know* 'im?"

He looked down. "I heard of him."

Since he was looking down at his porch, I couldn't tell if this was a good thing or a bad thing.

Mustard just went right on. "Well, he's here to help us find Ginny."

He looked up at last, but it was still a poker face. "He's the one to do it."

And I couldn't tell if *that* was an honest assessment or an ironic twist. I'm saying the guy was hard to read.

When in doubt, jump into the fire. If you get burned, you know better next time. I jumped. "We're in kind of a hurry, as you might imagine, but I was hoping to ask you just a few questions that'll put everything into perspective."

He held out open palms, a universal signal of acceptance. "Come on in. I've only got a minute. I want to get back out there."

We piled out of the truck and into the little house. It was dimly lit, and not as warm as the others had been. There was one big front room and the rest were dark. No offer of coffee. Just as well. I was getting a little jangly.

Dally and Mustard sat and made small talk. I asked if I might take advantage of his facilities. He gave me a curt nod down the hall. "First on your right."

I felt my way to the room in question. You know how in most bathrooms a person will have hand towels and little soaps or some kind of cleansing agent close to the sink, and often there'll be pictures and whatnot? Nothing of the sort for our boy Cedric. He was a no-nonsense kind of a guy. Just the facts. Bathroom tissue: check. Water: cold. Still, what caught my eye was the half-open medicine cabinet—with enough prescription bottles in it to lift a battalion of depressives.

I sauntered back out toward the living-room area. "What's with all the pills?"

He was not in the least offended. "Got shot a couple times."

I sat beside Dally. "Me too."

He raised his eyebrows. "Mine was in the line of duty."

I nodded. "Me too."

He kept his eyebrows up. "Really? Where?"

I shrugged. "Doesn't matter. I was in the service."

He smiled. "Me too."

Dally leaned forward and swiped at me with a casual hand. "We've really got no time for old war stories now, do you think?"

I nodded, looked around. "Nice place."

He sat back. "It's home."

"So, look—what's happened to Ginny McDonner, do *you* think?"

"Simple. She's out there lost in the woods. If she's not already dead, the snow and the cold—and another night out—will most likely take care of her. I came home for some warmer clothes and a bite to eat. I'm going back out again quick as we finish here. I'd feel a little guilty about spending too much time with you all . . . under the circumstances."

I nodded. "So I'm glad we caught you."

He breathed out. "What you need to ask?"

I gathered my thoughts. Might as well just blast. "Mr. Wicher ever been arrested? What happened to Ms. McDonner the year after Ginny was born? And . . ." I glanced over at Dally.

Dally jumped in. "Are Minister Dave and Ms. McDonner seeing each other?"

That quieted things down quite nicely.

I stepped into the silence. "Um, that's *her* question, not mine."

Mustard had to speak up then. "This the way you do it down in the city, is it?"

Good point. I shook my head. "Actually no. I'm usually a little more subtle. And you know your

cousin Dally to be exceedingly polite under most circumstances." I could hear my voice getting louder.
"But there's a little girl missing out there in the cold
and she's going to *die* if we don't move really fast. So
a lot of my boyish charm is cast aside in the urgency
of the moment. I swear to God, ordinarily I'm sweet
as honeysuckle, ask anybody. But desperate times call
for desperate rude-ass behavior. Wouldn't you
agree?"

Mustard looked at me. Tired as he was, I could see
he understood my sense of immediacy about the
whole thing. So I checked out the ex-Marine. He was
nodding his head.

"I agree—all except the cussing part. I feel it's im-
polite to use such language in the presence of a female
person under any circumstances."

But just as Dally was about to question the nature
of Cedric's possible sexual relationship with his own
mother, Mustard stood up.

I mean it was a *dramatic* moment. He shot up like
a rocket ship. You could actually feel the woosh of air
as he came to his feet.

I stood too. "Easy, big fella. What's up?"

Almost like he was in a trance: "The hut."

Dally said it first. "The what?"

He looked down at her, almost sick with revelation. "The hidin' place she had in the woods—the
Lost Pines Girl. I done tol' you'uns about it, the little
ol' tree hut made out of pine straw."

She remembered. "When you were a kid, they told
you it was still out there in the woods."

He blinked. "That's where she is." He closed his eyes. "I know she is."

Cedar was trying to look at all three of us at the same time. "What? What are y'all talking about?"

I filled him in. "The getaway place for the little ghost girl of Lost Pines—or whatever you'd call her. She ran off to a little place she'd made, or somebody's made. Mustard thinks it's still out there."

Mustard was holy with his vision. "They say it's like a little house. Ginny might be safe in there. She might be all right."

I barely had the heart to speak up. "That place isn't going to be there after all this time. Sounds more like wishful thinking to me, pal. Besides, wouldn't somebody have already checked this out? Like her folks?"

He shook me off, still in a kind of trance. "Don't nobody quite know where it is."

"Or even if it's out there at all. But." Cedar stood then, stared down at me. "You ever been hunting with Mustard?"

I shook my head.

He reached over on the chair where he'd been sitting and grabbed his coat. "He gets a feeling like this? There's bound to be game."

It was something I more or less had to go along with, given my own peculiar disposition toward the concept of *hunch*. "Okay, Cedar. Let's take your car. It'll seat all four of us and we can talk on the way."

We were out the door before he even had his coat on.

10

NIGHTSHADE

Dally in the front seat, Mustard and me in the back, Cedar shoving that beat-up Jeep through the night. Mustard gave direction. "Head for the old abandoned farm."

Dally turned around and patted his arm. "You okay?"

He nodded absently. "I get these feelin's." Softer. "I'm usually right."

Despite my fascination with Mustard's odd state, I saw no reason to abandon trying to get answers to my own questions. "So, *has* Wicher ever been arrested?"

Cedar kept his eye on the road, apparently knowing exactly which abandoned farm Mustard was talking about. "I recently locked him up for a spell."

"For?"

"Did you meet him?"

"Uh-huh."

Cedar was very neutral. "Exhibit any odd behavior?"

Dally ventured. "Like talking to his dead wife?"

Cedar kept his eyes on the road. "Here recently he's taken to telling everybody that he's been talking to the dead on a regular basis. I thought he might just need a little rest."

I wasn't sure what passed for "a little rest" in these parts. "So you put him, like, in the psycho ward around here?"

Cedar nodded. "He stayed over at the hospital for a spell. Seems better now."

I pressed. "Uh-huh. That all? Nothing else?"

He started to say something, then turned his face my way, eyes still carefully to the front. "Like what?"

"Loath as I am to be accused of ill manners once more tonight, I have to say he exhibited a tendency toward the . . . he seemed to have demonstrated what we all perceived to be a somewhat unhealthy appreciation for little girls."

In the same posture as before, Cedar spoke calmly. "You want to know does he molest children."

"More or less."

Cedar turned his face back again, squarely to the road. "Mr. Wicher is a lonely old man. There aren't that many of us who *wouldn't* exhibit a strange behavior or two under the same circumstances as he's had to live with."

I stayed shoved forward, my head nearly in between his and Dally's. "And yet I notice you do not entirely answer my question."

He nodded. "I do not."

The snow was really beginning to whip up, and it gave a false impression of light. Out of the corner of your eye you were tricked into thinking things were brighter than they actually were.

I sat back. "And what about Ms. McDonner? Anything you want to tell me about her?"

"She's not having an affair with the preacher, I'll tell you that. Her attachment to him is genuinely spiritual. You met the guy?"

"Dave? Not yet."

"David. And you come back and talk to me after you do. He's got something for you."

"*Got* something for me?"

"I mean for everybody. He's packed tight with the Holy Spirit."

I looked at the back of his head. "Are you also one of his flock?"

"Me? Naw. I'm an Episcopalian."

And that made all the difference. Now I understood more about just *who* was driving the Jeep. In the South, Episcopalians are the aristos—or think they are. The upper echelon. All the fun of being a Catholic and none of the guilt. I myself had, in fact, all the qualifications needed to be an Episcopal priest save the diploma—being that I was both divorced and serious about my wine.

Still, I was puzzled by Cedar's devotion to Minister Dave. "So why the affection for the guy?"

"You'll see when you meet him."

Dally pressed the next item on the list. "Ms. McDonner's pills. Why's she take 'em?"

Cedar spoke softly. "Nerves."

"So we've been repeatedly told." I stared at him. "What's she got to be nervous about?"

He started to say something again, then shook his head. "I don't believe it has anything to do with this situation. And it's also, by the way, none of your damn business"—glance to Dally—"sorry, ma'am."

She was about to let him have it right in his *sorry, Ma'am.* "Listen, *Buster* . . ."

But I saved him. "If it's got something to do with why she takes the pills that put her to sleep so she couldn't hear her daughter get up and leave the house? I think it's at least partially related to the situation at hand—wouldn't you say?"

He took a breath.

Mustard rallied himself from his state enough to help. "Cedar? Flap's got a sort of a God-given talent for findin' things. But he needs to know ever'thing. He's goin' to use what you tell him to find Ginny, see? You can't hold back on 'im—or we won't find Ginny."

I saw the first signs of caving. "Yes. I know his reputation."

I smiled. "Okay. So are you going to tell me the story—or not?"

"I don't know how this will help," Cedar began, tentatively.

Dally was the most impatient. "What *is* it?"

The Jeep slowed, just barely perceptibly, and Cedar's shoulders sagged. We had turned off the main road and were headed up a steep, rocky dirt track. My mind was stretching to come up with a new definition for the word *black.* I was trying to deal with the void-darkness in the woods on either side of the truck. Even the snow was hidden by the deep cave of night.

"If I tell you"—Cedar shook his head—"you have to say you won't spread it around. This is for *you* to hear—nobody else, right?"

I nodded big. "Who am I going to tell?"

He turned and actually looked Mustard in the face for a second. "You too, brother."

Mustard squinted. "You know me better'n that, boy."

He took a quick shot at Dally. "As you seem to want to be one of these modern women, Ma'am, I'll have to ask for your cooperation in this matter too."

She was stuck on terminology. "Modern women?"

He was suddenly at a loss. "Look, Ms. Oglethorpe. I mean no disrespect to you at all, and everything I say seems to rub you the wrong way. So you just take it from me that I don't mean to insult you, and I'll take it from you that you don't mean to be insulted. How about that?"

With a fair-sized breath, Dally agreed. "Right. I'll get over it. And I promise not to blab about Ms. McDonner—whatever it is that's her deal."

He was satisfied. "The problem is nerves. What's *caused* those nerves is the story."

The road got rougher and the Jeep slowed even more. We rounded a tough curve, and the headlights cut out across the black forest primeval. You could see eyes out there, honest to God. Could have been deer, could have been bear, could have been . . . almost anything, really.

"You might have noticed that Mr. McDonner is a touch older than his wife."

Dally couldn't keep quiet. "He's a *shove* older, if he's a day."

Cedar conceded. "Fifteen years. They were very happy when Ginny was born. They'd had more than one miscarriage. But when Ginny came along, the old man thought he could still have a family, see? So quick as Ms. McDonner got back on her feet, after Ginny came home, they got pregnant again. Only something went wrong, or was already wrong to start with. The baby had something wrong with it, is what I mean. Mr. McDonner couldn't handle it, so he . . . wanted his wife to take care of it."

Cedar fell silent.

Dally had to prompt. "Take care of it?"

Mustard helped. "Abortion, I b'lieve."

Cedar clicked his head. "You heard this before?"

Mustard looked out the window. "There's some that gossips."

Cedar looked away. "There's no such thing as a secret on *this* mountain."

Dally turned to look at Mustard. "She got an abortion? There was something wrong with the baby, so she got an abortion?"

He nodded. "Tha's what I heard. They say the baby mighta had that Down's Syndrome. And anyway, she didn't *get* th' abortion."

Cedar confirmed grimly. "I believe she did it herself."

Okay, that got me. "What?"

Mustard shook his head. "There really ain't no

such thing as a proper abortion up here. Even if there was, most people wouldn't do it. You got to go down to Atlanta—but there's other ways."

Dally was staring. "What did she do?"

Cedar had slowed the Jeep to all but a standstill. "There are some folk-style remedies that induce a premature labor."

Mustard nodded. "I heard it's got some belladonna an' some nightshade—mix it with saltwater . . . ain't sure of the rest."

My voice was a little low. "Belladonna and nightshade . . . those are poisons."

Mustard nodded again. "Sure enough."

Cedar's voice was even softer than mine. "All I know is I got a call about two in the morning from Mr. McDonner saying they had miscarried again and could I come take her to the hospital."

Dally shook her head. "He didn't call an ambulance?"

"Well, you can see how I live right next door, so I could get there quicker . . ."

I had to add, "Not to mention that maybe you won't ask the wrong questions."

He was harder again in his speech. "There's no law against having a miscarriage."

Dally wanted to get on with the story. "So you got there . . ."

He complied. ". . . and she was unconscious. She'd lost the baby and she was white as a sheet. We bundled her up and laid her out in the backseat. I flipped on the sirens and we were at the hospital in five minutes. I must have driven a hundred miles an hour."

I leaned forward again. "So what made you think it was something other than a miscarriage?"

He was trying to be all business. "Well, in the first place she was in her third trimester, so strictly speaking—"

Dally filled in. "—It was a premature birth."

He nodded slightly. "But the baby was dead and gone."

I fielded that one. "Gone?"

Cedar cleared his throat. "Mr. McDonner told me he'd already buried the little thing. Baby girl, he said."

"Baby girl." Dally looked away. "You didn't think that was kind of odd?"

"Sure I did, but the most important thing at that moment seemed to be getting to the hospital and keeping her alive. She was in a very bad way."

Dally sat back. "Go on."

"Doctors worked on her for hours. Wanted to know what she'd taken. They could see right away she had taken something, I guess. Mr. McDonner claimed not to know what they were talking about. They wanted to pump her stomach, but she'd already lost so much blood and so many fluids they were afraid to. Then, about dawn, she opened her eyes. The old man cried like a child. Maggie started in to praying just as soon as she could talk. The doctors said she was still under the effects of whatever medicine she'd taken. The prayers were . . . odd."

Mustard was calm. "Like what?"

"Something about a baby playing ball. Then something about a terrible punishment."

Mustard looked at me. "Belladonna nightmare."

Cedar shook his head. "No: Seven years a bird in the wood, seven years a fish in the flood, then a tongue in the warning bell, and seven years in the flames of hell."

Dally looked back at me. "What's he saying?"

But Mustard took a heavy sigh, like he'd just remembered something. "You know that tune. I done sung it for you before, remember?"

"What tune?"

"They's some that calls it 'The Cruel Mother,' but I call it 'Greenwood Side.' It's about a mother that kills her little baby with a penknife."

Dally beat me to this particular punch line. "What the *hell* are you talking about?"

Cedar elaborated. "It's a song."

I still wasn't clear. "She was singing a song in the hospital when she woke up? I thought you said she was praying."

He nodded. "It's probably on account of whatever it was she took to induce the labor—she had some hallucinations. She was talking out of her head."

Dally: "Such as?"

Cedar slowed the Jeep to a near stop. His voice was very flat. "Said she saw a little baby playing ball out in the yard, and it had no clothes on. And she said, 'If you were my little baby, I'd give you something warm to wear.' And the baby said, 'When I *was* yours, you left me cold and naked out in the woods.' And then she said she knew it was her own baby that she'd got rid of—ghost of her own baby. So she asked it what her punishment would be. And that's the part of the song about the seven years. It's all from the song Mustard was talking about."

Mustard blew out a little breath. "Man."

Dally wanted more. "So, this again made you somewhat suspicious, I'm hoping."

Cedar nodded. "Sure it did." He turned and looked Dally right in the eye. "But we never found the body of the little baby. You're a smart woman. I assume you understand the problem here."

She sat back. "No body, no crime."

He took his eyes off her. "More or less."

I looked at Mustard. "People don't still sing that song up here. It's, like, an old ballad."

He shrugged. "You'd be surprised. Foxfire, the Folk School—lots of kids are interested in the what-was."

Cedar was more to the point. "Even if we don't still sing the old-timey tunes every day, Mr. Tucker, there's a good number that knows about them, re-members them." He finally quit coasting and stopped the Jeep. "Just like a lot of kids up here are big Beatles fans."

That's right. You don't have to have been born in the milieu to dig it, to love it, to long to know it more.

Pine Straw

Dally looked out into the darkness. "Where are we?"

Mustard shoved open his door. "This here's the site of it."

"Site of *what*?"

"It's where the Little Girl of Lost Pines used to live."

We bundled up and stumbled out. Cedar had a searchlight-type lamp on the top of his vehicle. It scanned the night. Finally it fell on a barely discernible foundation and what was left of a stone chimney. On one side there was some cleared pastureland, maybe some fields; on the other, woods—lots of woods.

Mustard's voice was hushed. "That's where she used to live."

The snow was blowing in odd diagonal patterns and looked almost blue in the searchlight.

Dally matched her cousin's volume. "What are we looking for?"

Mustard started walking. "It's got to be 'round here some kind of way."

She looked at me. "What?"

I followed Mustard. "The *thing*. The legendary pine straw *hut*."

"Oh, right."

Cedar was still fussing with something in the truck. "Wait up. I got some flashlights."

He gave one to Dally, caught up with Mustard and me. I flicked mine on. It was like the high beam on a semi.

I smiled at Cedar. "Great flashlight."

He was unmoved. "We start here, we walk due north no more than fifty feet away from each other. Last thing in the world I need is to get you all lost too."

I agreed. "Good plan." I looked back at Ms. Oglethorpe. "I get to walk next to Dalliance."

Mustard piped up. "Me too."

Cedar nodded. "I'll take the outside."

We started walking, Dally and me in between Mustard and Cedar, all sweeping our big lights out in front of us like alien spacecraft looking for cows. We scared some deer pretty good, but otherwise there wasn't a sign of life. Anything sensible was inside a house or a hut or a warren or cave. Only the foolhardy ranged abroad on a night like that.

The woods could have been what they'd been before European settlers ever came to America. They could have been what they'd been before *human be-*

ings came along, for that matter. There were tall black trees and sloping rises, and the snow settled everything in a preternatural silence.

We must have walked north for an hour before Cedar changed direction. "Can't be this far away from the house, can it?"

Mustard shook his head, but he didn't say anything.

"Mustard," Dally prompted him, "can you let us in on your . . . intuition or whatever it is?"

He shook his head again. That's all.

So we headed east. It was blacker than black. Beyond the flashlight beam you couldn't see a thing. You'd think your eyes would adjust to the darkness after a while, but you'd be wrong. It just seemed to get darker.

Forty-five minutes' worth of east, and Mustard suddenly hooted. I mean *hooo*, like an owl.

Cedar hollered back. "What is it?"

"Somethin'."

There was a little dip, like a ravine, and Mustard was kneeling down in the snow over something. Dally got there first and just stared at it. I slipped in behind her. Cedar was there a second later.

What Mustard had found was a tiny human skull on top of a pile of large stones.

I couldn't help myself. "What the hell is this?"

Dally leaned back into me. "Looks like an altar or something."

Mustard reached out like he was going to touch it, then drew his hand back. "It's like a *baby* skull."

Dally nodded. "Yeah, that's *exactly* what it's like."

She turned around to look at me. "Another item in the 'too much of a coincidence' column."

My eyes were on the skull. "Absolutely." I glanced over to the constable. "You sure this thing's human?" But I already knew the answer.

"Sure. Look at it."

Mustard did just that. "Been here for quite some time."

It was just the top half, brown; the jawbone was nowhere to be seen. And sitting atop the stones as it was, it did seem like some kind of shrine or altar, not a burial place. I mean, in a burial place wouldn't the skull be on the *inside*?

Dally was obviously thinking along the same lines. "Could it be some kind of old Indian burial thing?"

Cedar shook his head. "Naw. Those are big burial *mounds*—earth mounds, and they're all put together sturdy. This is too . . . makeshift."

Mustard stood up. "This is some kids playin' around."

Cedar nodded. "Most likely."

I had to be the one: "But where'd they get the skull?"

Dally too: "And, you know, whose *is* it?"

Mustard started walking east again. "I'd have to say I'm more concerned about the livin' than the dead right at the moment."

I looked at Cedar. "We can't just leave this here . . . I mean . . ."

He took a deep breath and tilted his head in Mustard's direction. "I think I'd have to agree with *him*. This little thing is beyond our ability to help, but

Ginny McDonner is out *there* somewhere." He pointed his flashlight after Mustard.

The big boy called back to us over his left shoulder. "I b'lieve that thing there is a signpost. I b'lieve it means we close to the place we looking for."

Dally turned to Cedar. "Why would he say that?"

Cedar just started walking. "You *have* to go hunting with Mustard sometime."

A quick look passed between Dally and me, and then we followed after.

As we were pulling away from each other into our search positions, Dally whispered something odd to me. "Pretty little girls—one, two, three."

"Huh?"

She didn't look back at me, but she raised her voice a little. "The ghost of Lost Pines, the ghost of the *Greenwood Side* baby—and the ghost of Ginny McDonner. That's three."

I shined my light in her direction. "Not like you to wax pessimistic."

"I'm tired."

"Right."

She closed her eyes a moment. "And I'm just not in the mood to find a little girl's dead body."

"Well—me neither."

"I was . . . thinking about Sissy's little baby . . . and all . . ."

I started walking east. "Oh." But I had the idea I really didn't know *what* she was talking about. After that there was a general consensus of silence.

Another hour, and everything I had was cold. My hair was cold. My buttons were cold. I wanted a cup of hot coffee big enough to lie down in. I wasn't watching where I was going. I slipped on a mossy patch under the snow and slid down a little embankment. It was very embarrassing. Everybody noticed.

"Flap?" Dally came zipping down the slope like there were hundred-dollar bills at the bottom.

I was lying, up on my elbows, in a good drift of white. "I'm okay."

Mustard and Cedar hit me with their flashlights at the same time, and I was made blind. I shoved my arm up in front of my eyes and fell back into the snow.

Now, if you're a Christian sort of person, I'm told you really ought to believe in a little thing called Providence—divine direction. There's no other explanation for what happened.

As I fell back, my flashlight pointed up into the tree I had fallen next to. As it did, I saw the tree house. I was the one who saw it first because I was flat on my back, on account of being a clumsy dope. Everybody else was looking at me. I was looking at the tree house—and I couldn't get the words out.

"Uh, it's the . . . um . . ."

Mustard looked at Cedar. "Musta got the wind knocked out of 'im."

I flailed around trying to get up. "No. Look." And I pointed.

They looked, all four beams went up at once, and there it was: a big old tree house covered in pine straw, almost thatched. It was built at the nexus of two huge branches.

I guess it *could* have been anybody's tree house, up

in the air a good twenty feet. But we all knew—especially since we wanted so much to know—it was the object of our search. Or maybe it was the red jumpsuit we could all see hanging halfway out the door.

Dally's voice was thick. "Is that what I think it is?"

Cedar was already headed for the ladder. "I hope to God it is."

The ladder was only a series of flat boards nailed to the tree at kid-sized intervals. When Cedar put his big old boot on the first one, it let go of the tree right away, and the cop took a tumble.

I got to my feet. But before I could suggest anything else, Dally was flinging herself up the ladder. She was the best one for the job and we all knew it. The two local boys were just carrying too much excess baggage—too much Miss Nina's.

Dally made it up into the tree house in a snap. We had our flashlights trained all over the place.

She scooped up the jumpsuit on her way in—poked her head out a second later. "Nobody home."

Mustard looked down. Soft. "Nobody home."

I hollered up to her. "What's it like up there?"

"There's a bunch of *stuff*."

Cedar was itching to see it. "Like what? What kind of stuff?"

Dally disappeared back into the hut. "Want me to toss it down?"

He answered quick. "Yeah. Toss down the jumpsuit at least."

I took a deep breath. "I think I got to try to go up."

I had a shot. I was smaller than the other two, and

I thought maybe I could levitate part of the way up or something. I was thinking how, less than twenty-four hours before, I had seen Dally outside Mary Mac's and it'd made me think I could fly. All I needed to do now was fly straight up a couple of feet in the same direction: toward Dally.

"I'm coming up."

But she had already started her evacuation of stuff from the joint. The jumpsuit came raining down.

Cedar picked it up.

Mustard came over. "Is it hers?"

The cop checked. Nodded. "Got her name on the label. It's hers all right."

Mustard looked at Cedar. "Why you reckon she took it off?"

"Feel it. It's soaked. Rained a little last night, remember?" He called up to Dally. "There's other clothes up there?"

From inside she answered right back. "Lots."

I shoved myself up the first rungs. They shifted, but stayed. I was trying to think light thoughts.

About halfway up I had one foot on one board and another foot on another, and one of them gave way. Lucky for me the one I was holding on to with both hands stayed in place.

I made short work of the rest of the ladder and joined Dally in the little log-cabin home in the sky.

"Hey."

She turned around. "This place ain't big enough for the both of us."

"Says you."

"I swear to God, Flap, if this thing breaks and we

go crashing to the ground and die, I'm never speaking to you again."

"Fair enough." I sprayed my flashlight around the place. It was really quite sophisticated for a kid's tree house. Somebody, or several somebodies, had spent a lot of time and effort to make it a home. There were little kid lawn chairs and boxes for tables and three sleeping bags that I could see. There were pictures up on the walls, pictures some younger person had drawn. Sure, the place had walls. The wood was old, like barn wood, the cracks stuffed all through with pine straw. When I tapped the wood, it knocked solid. Same with the floor. Somebody had really put some work into the thing.

I couldn't stand. The ceiling was only five feet or so. I reclined on one arm and surveyed. "This is really something."

She pulled over a cardboard box full of clothes. "Look."

Sweaters, shoes, coveralls, hats, a scarf, and four or five mittens, all different, no pairs. I shuffled through it all. "Nice merchandise."

Mustard's voice interrupted. "What's goin' on up there?"

I answered. "Looks to us like the kid was here and got some better clothes."

"Better clothes?"

Dally stuck her head out the door and looked down. "There's a whole box up here. Want 'em?"

Cedar called up. "Yeah, toss down the box."

But before she could, Mustard interceded on behalf of the box. "Wait a minute. That's the . . . that stuff belongs to the kids, who-some ever fixed up the place. We best to leave 'at stuff be. You see how it helped out Ginny."

You had to admit he was right. This wasn't just a playhouse—it was a rescue station. Before Cedar even answered, Dally slid the box back where it had been.

I was still looking around. "Wonder how long this place has been here."

She sat still. "Think it's the place the Lost Pines girl came to?"

"You mean you think this *could be* the place?"

Shrug. "Could be, couldn't it?"

I didn't want to admit it. "I guess, but it sure looks well preserved."

"Why the reluctance, Mr. Coincidence?"

"I am not Mr. Coincidence."

"Really. Then who are you tonight?"

I was rubbing my hands to try to get some feeling back in them and thinking about borrowing some of the mittens. "I'm Mr. Coffee."

"You wish. Cold?"

"No thanks, I think I'm already gettin' one."

"Ah. Third-rate repartee. Like *that's* going to warm you up."

I blew on my hands. "Can I go home now?"

She was more serious. "No kiddin', how come you got reluctance all over you?"

I couldn't look her in the eye. "I got a bad feeling—I mean bad like . . . *strange*."

"How strange?"

"Strange enough to make me think there's lots

more at work in this neck of the woods than a missing little girl."

She headed for the door. "Aw, you're just spooked by the skull thing."

"You're not?"

She turned to me. "When we were kids, if we'd found a cool skull, you're telling me we wouldn't have done something like that, the little altar or whatever?"

My voice built. "If we were playing *Lord of the Flies,* maybe."

Again with the shrug. "I don't know. When you're a kid, skulls are just cool."

"Yeah, maybe . . . but it wouldn't have been enough to start me inventing my own religion."

Then she hit me with her sly look. It's so good she's got it patented. "So what was it that *did* start you inventing your own religion?"

She headed out the door.

I followed. "You gave me a book when we were kids, remember? A book, not a skull."

"That's all it took? That's all there was to it?"

I was crawling out onto the branch that went to the ladder. "Plus a trip to Asia and three songs by Van Morrison."

"Really. Which three?" She'd started down the ladder.

"Can't tell you—until you've gone through our initiation rites."

Mustard was impatient. "You'uns hurry on down. Ain't it cold up there?"

I answered. "Why, now you mention it—yes, it is cold up here."

Dally looked up. "There's nothing warming you up?"

I looked down. "Like?"

She looked away again, getting her footing. "Smell of pine straw."

And like it was a hurricane, a rush of a memory nearly knocked me out of the tree house. When Dally and I were kids playing in the woods, I happened to see her without her clothes on once. We were both about nine or ten, and she was about to go into a still part of the river where we used to play. I saw her, she saw me. Neither one of us moved. Then she smiled. "Want to go swimming?" I got out of my clothes before she was even finished with the sentence. We swam and splashed each other and threw each other around for maybe a couple of hours, then got out and let the sun dry us, lying in a bunch of pine straw. Ever since then the smell of pine straw . . . got to me. Can something be enticing and innocent at the same time? Anyway, I made the mistake of telling our Ms. Oglethorpe about the feeling once, and she's not one to forget.

Now that she'd reminded me, though, and I looked down at the tangle of her curly brown hair— the middle of the woods in the middle of the night with the temperature in the teens—and what do you know, I *did* stop shivering for a minute.

12

LONESOME ROAD

Down on the ground again we all just stood around a minute. Mustard was leaned up against a tree smoking a cigarette.

He was what they call downcast. "I really thought we'd find 'er here."

Cedar offered a little consolation. "We found her suit. We know she's all right."

He wouldn't have it. "Or *was*—when she changed out of it." He looked up. "We close to anything?"

Cedar looked around, trying to get his bearings. "We've got to be kind of close to the old logging road, don't we?"

The big boy thrust himself away from the tree, tossed his smoke into the snow. "That's right." He nodded his head in a northerly direction. "It should be over there."

I did my part. "Logging road?"

Mustard started walking. "It's pretty rough, but

we could follow it down the mountain. Lets out near the hospital, I b'lieve."

But Cedar had other ideas. "Abernathy, how long you been up—at this point?"

Mustard stopped and looked around at nothing in particular. "Couple days."

"Uh-huh. Don't you think you ought to get on back and rest up? You got a new baby coming home sometime soon."

He grinned. "I surely do." But he was stuck.

I could see then that he was so tired he was having trouble thinking what to do next. I shot a look to Dally.

She got it. "Hon? Why don't you an' me an' Flap just go on in now? Let the nice policeman do his job."

He still hovered, his eyes unfocused. "I . . . reckon I could sit down for a minute."

And sure enough that's just what he did, right in the snow, right where he was.

It took Dally and me tugging at him like a cartoon mule before he finally got up again.

He grinned. "I guess I'm a little more tired than I thought."

Dally patted his shoulder. "Let's go home, sugar."

"No. Take me to Sissy. Take me to the hospital. I got to see her an' the baby."

I let go of him. "Can you get the big boy there by yourself? I've got a powerful need to follow that logging road."

She stopped. "What?"

"I've got a feeling."

She nodded. "About what?"

"I don't know. But it's down there."

She squinted. "What's down there?"

I looked in the direction Mustard had pointed, toward the logging road. "Don't tell me you all of a sudden quit believing in my brand of intuition."

Cedar sidled up to us. "I can't let you go down that road—not by yourself. You'll get lost. And if we're taking Mustard to the hospital, I've got to drive. The Jeep is police property. So what we've got to do is *all* pile into it and let me drop you off. I'll finish up by myself."

But I wasn't listening. "We lose time that way. Why don't you take Mustard and Dally, I'll follow the road down to the hospital, you pick me up at the bottom, and we'll . . . see what we'll see. How lost can I get? I walk down, right?"

"Well . . ."

"I swear, if I start to walk up or sideways, I'll stop."

Dally looked at the policeman. "He gets like this. You just got to go with it. He's got the idea he knows something."

Cedar stared at me. "Does he?"

I stared back. "That's right, I know something."

There was a second there when I saw the cop look, the look in his eye that said he was going to cuff me and take me into custody. I have, alas, seen such a look on several occasions. As luck would have it, this look passed. It turned into another look I've seen a lot. It's one that says, *You're an idiot; what do I care if you get yourself into a whole lot of trouble?*

I smiled at him. "So, I'll meet you at the bottom of the mountain, by the hospital?"

"Don't go off the road for *anything*."

"Right."

"Don't touch anything you see."

"Check—unless it's Ginny."

He didn't think. "If she's still alive."

Dally and Mustard swiveled their heads toward him, and you could see right away he regretted saying it that way. Too late—and besides, it was what we were all thinking anyway—even though we hated thinking it.

I tried to save the day. "She's alive." It sounded certain. I wasn't—but I often win at poker. The others seemed fairly convinced I had a good hand.

Dally gave me a softer than usual look. "Take care. I don't feel like drivin' back to Atlanta myself."

Mustard was pretty far gone. "Where's Flap goin'?"

Cedar took his other arm. "To the hospital."

He nodded. "Okay. See you there, bud."

I nodded. "Check."

They started back for the Jeep.

I had to stop them. "Uh . . . just one thing?"

Cedar just shouted back without looking or stopping. "What?"

"Which way *exactly* is the logging road?"

He flashed a look that nearly collapsed the whole deal altogether. Then he made with the big sigh, and zoomed his flashlight in the direction away from the tree hut and the baby skull. "Over there. I'm going to stand here until you get on it."

I followed the beam of light over a little rise, and there it was: big, wide, deep-rutted; rough.

I called back. "Got it." Then, because I had to: "Now . . . I go *down*, right?"

He said something to Dally, but I couldn't hear what it was. Probably just as well. His light swung around, and I was on my own.

Just for laughs, I switched off my light. I wanted to see how things would be for Ginny. I thought my eyes would adjust after a minute. They didn't. It was so black, I was actually afraid I might run into a tree. No moon, no stars—at least the snow was letting up. Yeah, there was snow all around, and you'd think it would lighten things up a little, but, see, white only reflects light if there's actually light to reflect. I mean, it was almost as hard to see the ground as it was to see the forest. And the ruts in the road were big enough to park a foreign car in. I gave up after a minute, flipped the flash back on, down that lonesome road.

The trees were tall, I could tell that. Old trees, they've got a certain kind of feeling about them, a particular smell, maybe. The snow stopped, the wind seemed to die down. My feet were numb. I was wearing shoes you go to the nightclub in, not shoes to take a gambol through the primeval.

The fresh snow skunked any chance of seeing tiny footprints anywhere. All I could do was follow the road down and see where it took me.

Then, like flicking a switch, the clouds stepped aside and there was all kinds of moonlight everywhere. It was like somebody'd turned on a big silver searchlight. My flash seemed a little puny, so I popped it off. And before I could think to myself how beautiful and clear it all was, I saw two guys in business suits skitter between the clumps of trees off to my right, up the slope.

I ducked behind a pine myself, and peered out from behind it. Nothing. Maybe it had been a deer, or some hunters, or . . . maybe I was just getting nutty—cold-wacky.

I tried not to breathe. The air made little vapor ghosts every time I did. I was just about to step around in front of my hiding place again, feeling a little foolish in the grander scheme of things, when the two guys came slipping down the slope they were on. I think one of them was cussing.

Then I got the idea that maybe these were two more Samaritans, out looking for the little lost girl themselves. Only they didn't look very much like citizens of the locale. They looked like low-life street types—you know: they looked like me.

Dressed in suits and one guy had a fedora like mine, they both ended up sitting in the snow on their amusing little journey down the decline to the road. Down they were, and the smaller guy popped the other one pretty good in the arm. That guy shrugged, like he hadn't even felt it. Then he went into his coat pocket and pulled out a really big gun. Something automatic was all I could tell from where I was—not that I know much about firearms, truth be told. It's just that it wasn't a revolver.

He checked something, then slipped it back close to his heart. They both turned my way. They craned their necks, looking—then started toward me. Maybe it was just the way they were going.

Then: "Hey. Hey, buddy? Give us a hand, will you?"

Sure. I'd seen them, they'd seen me. Silly to hide like a kid, under the circumstances.

So I left the shelter of my hiding place. "Evenin', gents."

Even though I was a good twenty or thirty feet away, I startled the guys. Enough so that the bigger lug went for his pistol again.

I quick made with the international sign for surrender, hands halfway up. "Whoa back, pal. *You* asked *me* for help, remember?"

The smaller guy whacked the big guy again. "Put that damn thing away." Then he eyeballed me. "Hey . . . you ain't a local, are you?"

I put my hands down. "What gave me away? Was it the shoes?"

He cracked a smile. "Naw. It was the attitude."

"Right. I'm told I got to watch that."

He was all business. "So, the deal is, we're lost, we're tired, and we want to go to bed—and all kinds of 'show me the way to go home' comes to mind, do you get me?"

"Absolutely."

He turned to his companion. "See? At last a guy up here that speaks *English*." He turned back to me. "So what *are* you doin' up here, mind my axing?"

I shrugged. "Ax all you want—long as you can return the favor."

He pulled his head back from me in a little jerky

motion. "Oh. You want to know is what we got business up here?"

"Something like that."

He took a step closer to his friend. "Maybe it's the same business you got."

The big moose looked ready to draw again.

I decided to show my hand. "I doubt it. I'm up here looking for a little kid that's lost in the woods. Kind of a friend of a friend. Otherwise I'm just a tourist."

The moose spoke, but he seemed very nervous, like he was telling a lie. " 'At's what dem guys was talkin' about . . . before."

The little guy in the fedora explained it to me. "Yeah. That's right. See, we been out here all day an' night. We run into a number of your citizen locals looking all over sundry for the little tyke." Once more with the eyeball. "You don't look like the type, if you don't mind my sayin' so—get me?"

"Oh, I'm the type all right, I'm just not in my natural habitat."

"Which is?"

"Atlanta."

He nodded. "I see. Big city. You're just up here helpin' out a friend of a friend . . ."

"Uh-huh."

"An' I'm supposed to believe *this*?"

I smiled. "I guess you can believe what you want. They tell me this great land of ours was in fact founded on religious freedom."

He looked at Moose. "Hey, a comedian."

Moose was confused. "Really?"

I shook my head. "Look. I'm a kind of you-go-your-way-and-I'll-go-mine sort of a guy. Believe it or not, I *am* looking for a kid that's lost out here, one that's been gone a good long time at this point. So— much as I'd like to stand around and crack with the wise, maybe have a smoke with you two . . . or would that be *yous* two—I guess I'd have to say I got to be going."

The little guy was thinking. You could tell by the white steam coming up from his fedora. Then he turned to Moose. "Whatdaya think?"

Confused as ever: "Me? Uh . . ."

Fedora answered his own question. "Yeah. I can dig it." Looked at me. "See, we're in the way of bein' just a little bit lost ourselves. So can we help each other out? If you can get us in from the cold, we'll walk along with you to the nearest anything, make sure you don't fall down or nothin', and then be on our merry way. Ya know what I mean?"

I nodded. "As it happens, I'm going down this road, and it comes out by the hospital, they tell me. So if you feel like walking along and looking for a little ten-year-old, I'd actually kind of like the company." I popped on the flashlight again and showed it on the road. "Look out for the ruts. They're deep."

Moose was entranced. "Hey. A flashlight." He turned his big head to his cohort. "We coulda used that."

He gave his big friend a long-suffering look, obviously to be shared with me. "Yeah. That's right. We coulda used a flashlight out there in the dark for the last hundred and fifty hours."

I started down the road again.

Moose followed behind. "Was it that long?"

I looked back at the big guy. "Just keep your eye out for any signs of a little kid, okay? You know, clues."

He squinted, looked all about. "Yeah."

Fedora pulled in beside me. Honest to God, the guy was at least a foot shorter than me.

I let the flashlight play across the road. "So you never did tell me what *you're* up here for. I'm guessing not vacation."

That was a good one to him. "Are you kidding me? Vacation? Here? What's to vacate up here? *Vacation* is casinos and beaches, doncha think?"

"I don't know—I hardly ever take one. I'm usually the type to mix pleasure with a truckload of business."

He commiserated. "Tell me about it." He looked back at Moose. "When's the last time we had any real fun?"

Moose was quick. "This is fun."

He winked at me, Fedora actually winked. "See what I mean? Business *is* pleasure."

I looked back at Moose too. "And yet I notice you seem to be avoiding the issue, which is, what are you doing up here?"

Moose was wise. "Business trip."

I pressed. "What business?"

Moose answered. "Real estate."

That stopped me. "Real estate?"

Fedora kept on walking. "More like land acquisition."

Moose indicated with a flutter of his ham-hand that I should keep moving, so I marched on.

Fedora was happy to gab. "You got *big* room up here. Plus you got a *little* economy. Let us say that a factory wants to get built up here. You got, right away, a gaggle of goons that needs the work and is going to do it for kind of cheap—at least until some union or other gets ahold of 'em. Plus you got all manner of distractions for the executive types: big houses that overlook big valleys, lakes for the fishin' an' . . . whatever the hell else it is you do in a lake. Boats, I guess. Anyhow, everybody's happy . . . *if* you get the land *and* you get it at the right price." He lowered his voice. "Trouble is, the people up here, they're suspicious of outsiders comin' to take their land. And Pappy Yokam don' want to sell the homestead. Plus he's got a inflated idea of what it might be worth. So, to make a long story somewhat shorter, we—my large colleague an' me—we help acquire the land."

I looked back over my shoulder. "That right, Moose? You're a robber-baron?"

"Huh?"

Fedora smiled. "You're confusin' him. He ain't never robbed nobody in his life. An' his name ain't Moose."

I nodded. "I just call him that."

Moose seemed far away for a second. "My brudder used to call me Moose. I ain't seen him in a montha Sundays."

I wanted to know. "Where's he living now?"

He was happy to oblige. "Rockford, outside Chicago."

I smiled. "Nice little town, is it?"

"Not so little."

I smiled bigger, so he'd know I was friendly. "Not if your brother's big as you, it's not."

Moose cracked a grin himself. "Me? I'm the runt."

Fedora interrupted. "We through with family hour, here?"

I looked back at him. "So you two help convince the population hereabout that selling their land would, ultimately, be . . . healthier than not selling."

He was very serious. "We're businessmen. Occasionally somebody might get the wrong idea about us, an' feel a little intimidated—might feel we got a notion to strong-arm. But, like I say, that's the wrong idea. We're *business* types, get me?"

I shrugged. "Yeah."

I was about to press for more information about just who it was might want to buy land around Lost Pines, when Moose halted dead in his tracks, grabbed my arm, and spun me around to my right.

"Look! Clue!"

His hot-dog finger was indicating something important to him in the woods. I played the light that way, and what do you know: There *was* something. Looked like a little kid's wool hat.

Fedora flashed him some kind of look; seemed, maybe, mad or something. I thought he might be perturbed at the notion of slowing our progress toward someplace warm, but Moose just looked suddenly like he'd made a mistake.

As for myself, I had to congratulate him. "Nice work, pal. I think it actually might be something, and shame on me for not seeing it first."

He was modest. "I got good eyesight."

We all stumbled over to it. As it was on top of the snow, see, and the snow had just quit, we imagined it might have been a recent deposit. I scooped it up. It was little—definitely a tyke chapeau.

Fedora was in a musing kind of mood. "Uh, course it could be *any* little kid's hat."

I nodded. "Any little kid that'd be up at this time of the night. It's pretty late for hide an' go seek, or what have you."

Moose looked around like he was telling time by staring at the trees. "Yeah, I guess it *is* kind of late at that."

I went on. "And we did track the kid in question up to this general locale—we think."

Fedora looked around. "What is this, the *royal* we? I don' see nobody but us chickens."

I nodded. "My troops. They're waiting for me at the end of this very road."

He smiled. "Is that right? More urban sophisticates such as yourself?"

"Naw. Locals mostly." I didn't feel like mentioning that one was a cop. Seemed like it might make them nervous, and they appeared to be a little nervous just to hear that there were other night crawlers like us out and about. Being in their particular line of work, I could see why.

Fedora looked around. "Let's get on with it. There's no findin' the kid from just looking at her hat."

Cold as I was, my brain was still cooking enough to get ahold of something wrong in that sentence. It only took me a second to figure out what it was. "How'd you know the kid, the lost kid, was a girl?"

He didn't look at me. He looked at the hat. "You tol' me."

I shook my head. "Try again. I'm big on gender neutrality in language."

He still wouldn't give me a gander. "Musta been those other guys, the ones we run into earlier who was lookin' for 'er too."

Moose erupted. "Hey!"

I shot him a look, but so did Fedora, and the big guy got very quiet again, all of a sudden.

I still tried. "What?"

He looked down. "Nothin'. I just thoughta somethin', is all."

"What was it?"

"I just remembered . . ." And he looked over to Fedora. "I just remembered I ain't had no dinner an' I'm kind of hungry."

"Maybe they got a cafeteria at the hospital down there," Fedora pushed.

Moose seemed disappointed. "I hate hospital food."

He said it like a guy who'd spent some time in a hospital.

Fedora was building on a good mad. "Look. You guys can stand here in the ice an' snow an' whatnot all night long if you want to. Me? I'm headin' on down the road. Get me?"

Moose nodded.

I held my ground. "She could have just dropped this. She might be right here, right close . . ."

But I didn't even get a chance to finish my thought. Fedora nodded. Moose drew. It was a big old automatic, sure enough.

Fedora was very polite. "The three of us is all goin' down the hill. I'm not going to be stuck out here in the cold anymore, and you're just the guy to get me out of it. Now, I apologize right this minute for slappin' a pistol into the proceedings, but necessity is a mother here in this particular case. Don't be angry with me. Let's just go on down the road."

I looked at Moose.

He shrugged. Then he leaned in close to me. "I ain't really going to shoot you. Dis is just to give you some kind of scare."

Caught, as I was, on the horns of a big mean dilemma, I acquiesced. Ginny had warm clothes, and she seemed to know where she was going better than anybody who was trying to find her. I actually felt better about her chances than I did about mine at that moment.

I smiled politely at Moose. "Okay."

He put the gun away.

I pocketed the hat as best I could, broke off a nearby pine bough and stuck it in the snow where we'd found the hat, and down the road we went.

It was crummy going, and I realized that these guys were more or less under the impression that they were escorting me down the hill, and that my sole purpose in life was to get them out of the woods. It was a clear case of the blind leading the stupid.

With no more snappy conversation, we trundled our way just fine until we saw some lights ahead.

Fedora stopped. "What is it?"

I peered. "Cars on the road?"

He breathed out. "Yeah. Yeah, that's it. Cars."

Moose smiled. "We ain't lost no more."

I smiled back. I really wanted the guy on my side. "That's right, bud."

We made it down the rest of the old logging road with very little ado. The lights, as it turns out, were some parking-lot lights. We were in back of the Wal-Mart. You could see the hospital a little way off in the distance. Much to my dismay, given the tenor of our relationship, Cedar's cop-mobile was nowhere to be seen.

I picked up the pace. "So, gents. Welcome to what passes for civilization around here. You want to come meet my friends, or is this good-bye for us?"

Fedora was looking down the road. "Which way is back to town?"

I shrugged. "I don't know." I pointed down the road away from the hospital. "That way, I think."

Fedora gave me the strongest once-over I think I'd ever gotten. "You don't seem like the type that gets all bent out of shape by one little face-to-face with a firearm. I'm countin' on your ability to forgive an' forget." He stepped closer to me. "Plus, I got a real good memory for faces." Then he flashed a very winning smile. "We'll be catchin' you on the flip side."

Moose grinned. "That means 'See you later.' He loves talkin' that way."

I nodded. "I'm hip."

He started off after his other half. "See you 'round."

I watched them go. I was pretty sure I'd see them again, and soon. "I'm countin' on it."

And then they were gone. Strangers in the night. Do be do be do. I must have been getting pretty tired, at that point, to have *that* in my head. Still, there it was, and I was hiking with all my might toward the hospital, Dally, hot coffee, warm feet, and a little woolen prize to share with all and sundry, tucked nicely away in my coat.

13

HATS

Hats used to be all the fashion. Now they seem more a statement than a matter of course. You don't assume a hat anymore, you don one deliberately. In the big city a wool hat means something other than it means in the country. It's my opinion that this odd and somewhat lax view of headwear started with President Kennedy. Wasn't he the first to be inaugurated bare-pate? And wasn't it even snowing? After a cue like that the whole nation started in to giving all manner of haberdashery the once-over. My own somewhat arcane chapeau has, on occasion, been the object of derision. I don't care. Ultimately I believe hats have a single purpose in this life. When somebody asked the Dalai Lama the meaning or religious significance of the thing he wore on top, he tilted it a little and said only, "It keeps my head warm."

The hospital was very calm and quiet. Even the nurse at the maternity ward seemed to be dozing just a little. I smiled at her as I walked past. Without even opening her eyes she said, "Don't wake Sissy or Mustard up, they need their sleep. The others are down by the coffee machine."

How she knew who I was or what I was doing there, how she even saw me through closed eyelids, I wouldn't know.

Still, there were Dally and Cedar at the coffee machine, and they waved when they saw me coming.

Cedar spoke right up. "That was quick. We were just about to head over to the Wal-Mart parking lot."

Dally offered me a cup. "I think you'll find this the worst coffee you ever tasted."

I took it. "Doesn't matter. I got news."

Cedar squinted. "You find something?"

"Oh, yeah."

I produced the wool hat like it was a rabbit out of a hat. They were both impressed.

Cedar took it. "Could be something."

I nodded. "It was on top of the snow. No snow covering it."

He understood right away. "Snow just stopped. This is a recent loss."

"Right."

He really gave me the eye. "Why didn't you stay out there looking? Why'd you come in?"

I looked at Dally. "I had company that sort of forced me out of the woods."

Cedar spoke first. "What?"

But Dally was a close second. "Other folks out looking?"

I shook my head. "Not folks. Hoods. City types."

Cedar folded his arms. "Doing what?"

"Being lost, far as I could tell. I rescued them."

Dally could tell I was keeping something back. "What're they doing up here?"

I looked at Cedar. "Said they were in the real estate business."

He looked at the floor. "BarnDoor."

Dally and I both waited for more.

She finally looked at him. "What?"

"BarnDoor, Limited. Got to be. It's a kind of designer home-improvement company, sells fieldstone, lumber, old barn wood, clay bricks . . . they want a factory sort of a deal up here. That's got to be what they meant."

I still didn't get it. "What kind of a factory?"

He was still looking at the floor. "They want to take the fieldstone and the lumber and the other resources and package them in a high-end kind of way. Mail order, mostly. You buy an old barn up here from some needy farmer for a hundred bucks, then you package it just right and you sell each board for twenty-five. It's quite a profit."

Dally grinned at me. "Big money in home improvement."

I shook my head. "I don't see these guys I was with tonight being associated with a happy yuppie organization of that ilk."

Cedar turned quite the calloused gaze my way. "Business, Mr. Tucker. No heart, no soul, no conscience. BarnDoor's had several unsavory types up here hassling people to sell. That's what big-city business is all about."

I returned the look. "You seem a little young to be quite so bitter, if you don't mind my saying so."

He looked away again. "People up here? We . . . things get taken from us without our knowing it. Land gets grabbed. Beautiful valleys where homes used to be are turned into lakes for the summer tourists. People from the city think our poverty is *quaint*. The way we talk is a little joke to them. Our suspicion of outsiders is crafted from experience, not a natural predisposition."

I shrugged. "Maybe. But you don't have a corner on the market. Everybody and his brother thinks in terms of *us* and *them*. It's the main thing that makes the world a more difficult place than it needs to be."

He actually smiled. "That sounds like David."

I smiled right back. "Really? Gotta meet the guy."

Dally jumped in. "I was thinking the same thing myself. How about a little shut-eye and a visit to Preacher Dave in the morning?"

Cedar finished his rotten coffee. "I might like to go back up there and look harder for Ginny where Mr. Tucker found this cap."

I nodded. "I stuck a pine branch where we found it. I might need to show you, though."

Dally took my arm. "*If* it came from Ginny, seems like she might be doing all right at the moment. Why don't we just let Officer Duffie go up there and look. You and I? We're going to get some sleep."

I sighed. "Now you're talking to me like you were talking to Mustard to get him to come here to the hospital."

"Right."

"And by the way, how's Sissy . . . and the baby?"

"All's well. They're all fast asleep. Everybody in town's asleep but the three of us."

I thought about my recent acquaintances. "Not everybody."

She ignored. She looked at Cedar. "Where are we going to find a place to crash at this time of night?"

It only took him a second. "Miss Nina's got some cots out in the room behind her kitchen. It's real warm. I'll leave her a note." He glanced at his watch. "She'll be up in an hour or so. I'll tell her to try and not wake you up."

Dally cranked up the charm. "Thanks." She touched his arm.

It worked. He blushed. "Sure thing."

We were lying down inside twenty minutes. Miss Nina's pantry was bigger than most hotel rooms, and it opened out onto a back porch, where Cedar had let us in. He seemed to have keys to everything in town. He went to put a note on Miss Nina's door, and then to see if he could get his Jeep up the logging road. I'd done my best to describe the location of the hat discovery. I still felt I ought to go with him, but Dally was so insistent on my not doing it that I figured she wanted to talk.

There were three cots. The pantry was warm and dark and silent. The cots were thick with homemade quilts and feather pillows, but I was still wearing my coat. I was thawing out. I was very happy. I was drifting off.

But Dally, as I had suspected, had other ideas. "So now what's the deal with these goons from BarnDoor—if that's where they're from at all? And what's with the strange sensation you had that made you stay out in the cold and go down the logging road? Spill."

My eyes were closed tight, but Dally's voice made a kind of candlelight sensation in my head. "I knew there was something out there."

"You knew the goons were there?"

"Not exactly."

"The hat? The kid?"

"Nothing that specific. It was a feeling, like."

She hesitated. "You going to do your thing? Your trick?"

"Here? Now? Naw. I've got to be rested up, I can't be falling asleep. Plus, you're too distracting. I've got to be alone."

"I'm distracting?"

I smiled in the darkness. "Constantly."

She shifted in her cot. "Huh."

She knew I couldn't do my trick with her in the room. The trick takes concentration, balance, and maybe a little more information. It wasn't time for the trick yet.

I sighed. "That's not all you wanted to ask."

Beat. "No."

"Then?"

She cleared her throat, like she was going to make

a speech. "I just wanted to talk it out, you know. I've got to say I think Wicher did it."

"Did what?"

"I think he's got Ginny. Or he's the reason she's gone."

I turned on my back. "Really? Then what were we doing out in the cold all night?"

"I think she got away. I think he snatched her, and she escaped, but she was afraid to go home."

"Afraid?"

"Because her mom takes all those pills and her dad iced her sister."

I opened my eye. "She doesn't know any of that."

"Yeah, probably not. I'm just thinking out loud, really. Want me to shut up?"

"No. You *know* how you say things in a conversation like this, things you didn't even think you knew. I like this."

"Me too."

I closed my eyes again. "Still, Wicher is a fairly prime suspect in my own thinking at the moment."

She yawned. "Check."

"And the pills and the dead sibling, they've got something to do with all this." I yawned.

"Ya think?"

I rolled over. "Plus, there's a lot more to Cedar Duffie than meets the eye."

"Oh, I'm convinced of *that*. The diction alone . . ."

". . . is too *Marine*?"

I could tell she smiled. "Or something. And what about this Preacher Dave?"

"Yeah, I've got to meet him."

"I want to see 'em pick up the snakes."

I was drifting. "Mm-hmm."

Her voice was very soft. " 'Night, Flap."

"Sweet dreams, kiddo."

And we were both out before we took another breath.

14

FOOD

Twenty minutes later I was awake. Okay, maybe it was longer than that, but that's about how rested I felt. What with the rattling of pots and pans and the sizzling of this and that, I was out of dreamland and into the world of too much coffee again.

I sat up. Dally was still out. She could sleep through an avalanche. I slipped out of bed and peeped through the door. There was Miss Nina, making with the country cuisine.

I entered her kitchen as politely as I could; nodded. I was still wearing my heavy coat, but it was giving new meaning to the word *rumpled*.

She nodded too, turned away, and when she came back, there was a little tray with sausage biscuits and a mug of coffee on it. She shoved it my way. I took it. Words were unnecessary. Would have been utterly superfluous.

I made my way into the dining area. There were all

manner of locals wreaking havoc on grits and red-eye gravy. They took little notice of me. What's more important, after all, a goofball stranger or fine dining? They were also distracted by some other dapper out-of-towner who was making with the hearty farewell.

"Bye, y'all. See you tonight!" He was smiling to beat the band. Nearly everybody in the joint was ignoring him. City folk.

I took a seat at an empty table, slugged back some of the coffee, burned my tongue, and plowed into the first biscuit. I was midway through the third or fourth chew when the guy at the next table spoke up.

Without looking my way, he made himself known. "You Tucker?"

I kept on chewing.

He insisted, a little louder. "I say, you Tucker?"

I swallowed. Kept a tight gander at the rest of my breakfast. "Ordinarily I'd be *Mr.* Tucker in a situation like this. But since I've just about *had* it with the introductory behavior of all and sundry here about"—I turned up my own volume just a notch—"because you all seem to be unacquainted with a little thing they invented called *manners*—I'll just pretend I have no business with you at all and finish my food, okay?"

He seemed amused. "Cedar *said* you was a mean 'un."

"He was right."

"He also said you were going find Ginny McDonner. Done that yet?"

I blew on the coffee, took another sip. "Found her

hat. Found her little red jumpsuit." I shot him a look.
"And while you were home, I'm assuming, *asleep* last
night, I was roaming down that logging road out
back of Wal-Mart trying to help out. So excuse me if I
seem a little mean, but I got no sleep, and no time to
chat. You finish your grits. I'm going to go get me a
little kid."

Just for emphasis I swallowed the rest of the biscuit whole, tossed back all of the coffee, and stood.

His voice only got sunnier. "Why would you want
to be so riled this early in the morning?"

I looked at him good then. "One of the very best
things there is about the South is the manners. It's not
an affectation, it's a way of life. Southern gentility is
something for the rest of the world to learn. I don't
much care for your wreckin' the curve."

"What?"

"I've visited in this county before, and it's behavior
like yours that makes the rest of the country think
that *Deliverance* wasn't just a movie."

He went back to his grits. But he smiled. "It
wasn't. It was a book first. James Dickey, the Original Buckhead Boy, the poet."

That gave me pause. "Okay—you got me there."

He smiled even bigger. "Have to admit you've got
me too . . . Mr. Tucker. Had no intention of being
rude. Sorry it seemed like it." He offered his hand.

I took the few steps over to his table, stuck out my
hand. "Maybe I'm a little too quick to jump into it
myself."

He looked me in the eye. He was quite the clear-eyed gentleman after all. "I'm David." He tipped the brim of his cap. "Came to talk with you."

"You're Preacher Dave?"

That smile just kept getting bigger. "David."

"Right."

"And did you know . . . Won't you have a seat?"

I sat.

He went on, kind of a fast talker. "And did you know that in most polite English-speaking societies, the use of the last name without the formal address is actually considered friendlier than anything else, until you're on a first-name basis with the acquaintance. Are we on a first-name basis?"

I nodded. I was impressed with the precision of his speech given the speed of it. "Since you don't seem to have anything else *but* a first name, I'd be okay with it."

He finished his grits. "Your first name's Flap, they tell me. What kind of a name is that?"

"It's the word that most accurately describes the relationship between my parents."

"I see. Although you were something of a trouble-maker yourself at one time, I'd imagine."

I shrugged. "You can imagine anything you like."

He slid the plate away from him. "You didn't get enough sleep last night." He looked at my clothes. "And you're not dressed for trompin' around in the woods much, are you?"

"Everybody wants to criticize my threads."

He shook his head. "They don't *want* to, they *have* to."

"Oh, really?"

He let it drop. "Cedar said you'd want to talk to me. I thought I'd oblige—and get breakfast in the process. A waste of time is worse than an insult to God."

"Ah, now come the pithy religious bon mots, I'm guessing."

He just kept on with the smiling. "Oh, some are much more long-winded than pithy. I can go on quite a stretch when I get wound up."

"I don't doubt it. Slug back a little lye and you're bound to have a few things on your mind that bear expressing."

He nodded. "I'm more of a battery-acid man myself."

I just shook my head. "Brother."

He winked. No kidding. "All a part of the show."

I thought I was wise. "Show, huh?"

But he didn't want me to misunderstand. "No. Not like show *business*. I mean the Big Show."

"Big Show?"

He looked around the room, but he seemed to be looking around the universe. He held out his hands. All of a sudden his face was angelic. And I'm not lying, the whole joint seemed a little brighter. Whatever it was, I got the picture. The *Big* Show.

I was a little unsteadied, but I didn't want him in on it. "Nice nonverbalization."

Still with the face. "If you can say it in words—it's not it."

All I could do to that, of course, was nod.

I was just about to get into some serious prying, when the door to Miss Nina's nearly came off its hinges, and Cedar Duffie blew into the room like a man on fire.

"Flap!"

"Cedar?"

"Now!"

And he was back out the door.

I looked over to David. "I've got a lot more to hear from you."

He nodded. "Amen."

15

DAYS

Cedar's Jeep was already starting to roll back out into the street as I was climbing in the passenger side. He looked wild.

I slammed the door. "What?"

"Old man Wicher."

"What about him?"

"He's gone. I went over to ask him a few questions of my own—and he's flat gone."

I blinked. "Gone?"

"Bunch of stuff cleared out from his house, including the toys and all for Ginny, and nobody knows where he is. You all were the last ones to see him—last night."

"Couldn't he just be . . . I don't know . . . shopping, or out in the fields or . . ."

"He hardly ever leaves the house. He . . . he says he doesn't like to leave his wife alone."

"So you think . . ."

He nodded very heavily. "I think he's fled with Ginny McDonner."

We made it to Wicher's house in under five minutes, despite the snow in the streets. The front door was unlocked.

Cedar poked his head in. "Mr. Wicher? You in here? It's Officer Duffie."

I noticed that. Not *Cedar* Duffie.

After another couple of seconds he turned to me. "See?"

I shook my head. "I'm still not convinced this is anything. The guy might be out for a walk, even. Or maybe he got up early to help us all *find* the little kid."

Cedar looked at the floor. "All I can say is that it's not like him. You yourself pointed out last night how strange you thought he was."

He stepped over the threshold.

I followed. "I have to admit, Dally and I were thinking he was the one . . . Shoot."

"What?"

"I left Dally asleep over at Miss Nina's. She won't know what's what."

He took another few steps. "David'll wait for her. He'll tell her what happened to you."

"He will?"

"He wants to talk to her."

"About what?"

"Sissy's new baby, he said—or somethin' about a baby."

I followed him into the inner sanctum, toward the sitting room. "What about it?"

He just shrugged.

We were in the room where Mustard and Dally and I had been the night before, but all the litter that had been on the floor, the whittling and the toys and whatnot—all that was gone. The room was spic and span.

I looked around behind the chair the old man had sat in, just to make sure. Everything was gone. "I see what you mean."

He tilted his head. "Same thing upstairs."

"Meaning?"

"Not everything, but some clothes, toothbrush, razor—all gone."

I nodded. "So he's not out hiking."

He looked very worried. "I should have kept a better eye on the old guy. I mean, I knew he was . . ." But he couldn't finish his sentence.

I looked at him. "Still . . . seems like a big jump to think he's got Ginny."

He wouldn't look at me. "Probably right. I just want . . . I want something more than a wool hat and a vague hope to go on."

"Me too," I told him. "Feel like going back over to the McDonners'?"

"What for?"

"Now that my head's a little clearer, what with the three hours' sleep and the weak coffee in me, I got a couple extra questions for 'em. About the night Ginny disappeared."

"I feel a necessity to poke around here for a minute, maybe scare up something that'll tell me where Wicher is. Maybe even find something of Ginny's."

I lifted my shoulders again. "Don't go jumping to any conclusions. She was over here a lot. Probably some of her stuff here from her normal visits."

He was icy. "I'm unsure, now, if there were ever anything like *normal* visits to this house."

"I see."

"Why don't you just hike it over to the McDonners'? I'll come by in a minute, after I've had a good look around here."

"Sure. I really didn't get enough of walking around in the snow last night."

He was irritated. I was guessing he hadn't gotten any sleep at all. "Fine, then have a seat and wait for me to finish up here."

I finally figured out what it was about the guy that made me a little uneasy. Everybody else I'd met up in Lost Pines was what you might call a character. Cedar had nothing of the sort in his own makeup. He was absent any distinguishing marks—or remarks. He was Marine stiff and government-issue bland. He was the most normal, boring guy in the community— which, in the very oddest of ways, made him unique in his environment. There had to be something under that tight surface. But I was more interested in other puzzles at that moment.

I pulled my coat around me. "Nope. Think I'll walk on over to the McDonners'. You'll come get me?"

He nodded, headed toward the stairs.

I watched him ascend, then I popped open the front door.

The air was clear outside. Seemed like it was finished snowing. Still plenty of clouds, but they didn't seem tough.

I had to think for a second which way to head, but once I got my bearings, I was certain of the way to walk. I decided to trudge down the main road. Seemed like that would be easiest going.

It wasn't long before the road curved and the McDonner place was up in front of me. Even in the new-fallen snow, I could tell where Mustard's truck had torn up a part of the landscape. I stood there awhile, breathing in the clean air and staring at the place on the road where Ginny had been, playing in the middle of the road in the middle of the night. That's what I wanted to know about.

I was halfway down the driveway when Mr. McDonner came out on the porch.

"That you, Mr. Tucker?"

I called back. "Sure is. Mind if I talk to you for a minute?"

"You find anything?"

"Not much—but it's something. You haven't spoken to anybody this morning?"

"About what?"

I was nearing the porch, and we lowered our voices. "Nobody told you? We think we found her jumpsuit and maybe a wool hat she was wearing."

He stared out toward me.

"Yeah. Mustard had the idea she might be over at the old abandoned farm."

"Abandoned farm?"

And I realized at that very second I had no idea what the ghost girl's last name was. "You know, where the ghost of Lost Pines used to live. What was their name, the moonshiner and his family and the little girl and all?"

He got softer. "They was Rayburns."

"Well . . ." I climbed the two steps up onto the porch. "That's where Mustard took us last night. Good thing too. We found some old tree hut where the kids had been playing. We think Ginny went there and changed clothes and got a hat. So . . . you know . . ."

He whispered. "She's alive."

"I don't want to get up any false hopes, but at least she made it up there to that place and was feeling good enough to climb up a tree."

Even softer. "She's alive."

Mrs. McDonner was all of a sudden out on the porch with us. I guess she'd been standing at the door. "Ginny's alive?"

I took a shot at being the voice of reason. "Let's not get too specific . . ."

Mr. McDonner looked at his wife. "She was up at the place . . ." He gave a look to me, then went on. "She was up at the old Rayburn place."

She looked at me, very strangely. "What was she doing up there?"

I smiled. "I don't know, ma'am. Actually—I was thinking maybe you'd tell me."

She looked away. "Come on in the house, Mr. Tucker."

Her husband let me go first. I followed her, he followed me.

The house felt hot to me after my hike in the snow. I got out of my coat right away.

The missus was headed right for the kitchen. "You had any breakfast yet, Mr. Tucker? You hungry?"

I smiled. "I'm riding on Miss Nina's biscuits."

That made her smile too. She agreed. "They gets good mileage. Coffee?"

"Sure."

We all sat down in the kitchen. I draped my coat and hat over an empty chair. I was starting to sweat.

Mr. McDonner started to talk. "You say it was Mustard's idea to go up to the old Rayburn place?"

The way he said it, made it sound like a strange choice. But he seemed to be trying too hard, for some reason.

I nodded. "Good thing too. I believe that's where she was, up there—only a few hours ago."

Mrs. McDonner dropped the spoon she was bringing me. She started to cry, like a kid who's spilled something on the table.

Mr. McDonner got up. "It's all right, sweetheart. It's going to be all right."

I didn't know what else to say. "I found a wool hat on the logging road up behind Wal-Mart. You know the one? We think she was wearing it."

Mr. McDonner sighed. "Where'd she get it?"

"We think she got it, along with a change of clothes, in a little tree hut up there on the property. Did she ever mention going there, like to play or anything? Maybe with some other kids? Looked like a kind of playhouse for a bunch, not just one."

Mrs. McDonner forgot her coffee. She sat down at the table with us. She stared at that nice Formica tabletop. "We know the place."

Her husband jumped. "Darlin' . . ."

But she shot him a look like a crow on a rooftop: black and menacing.

He sighed again.

I've noticed that people who spend a lot of time working hard, especially on the land—hard jobs, isolated lives—fall into two categories linguistically speaking: those who seem to think that words are too strange and difficult to bother with, and those who think words ought to be scattered like broadcasting seed. Some find it hard to talk at all, in short, and some can't shut up. The McDonners fell into the former category, obviously.

Finally the old guy looked at me. "Rayburn? He was a no-good. A drunk. Beat his own wife an' child. That fire that burned him up? It was a clear retribution of the Lord. It's just too bad . . . it's too bad the wife died too."

Mrs. McDonner finished the thought. "She was a Day . . . like me."

I shook my head. "You mean some of your kin was the mother of the Little Girl of Lost Pines?"

She couldn't look me in the eye, but she nodded. "Christy. She would have been Ginny's second cousin, I believe."

"Her mother . . ." I had to think. ". . . your mother . . . ?"

"There was fourteen kids in their family."

My brain has always been a sieve as far as genealogy goes. "Never mind. Suffice it to say, you're related."

He nodded. "That property's deeded to us."

I snapped my head up so hard it made my hat fall off the chair beside me. "The abandoned farm belongs to *you all*?

He nodded.

She elucidated. "We go up there ever' so often. Picnic. Play. It's real pretty in the fall—leaves an' all . . ." And she drifted off thinking about it.

He added, "So she knows the place quite well. That tree hut? It must have been up there for years. Somebody's fixed it up recently—looks like. Don't know who. But some of the kids play up there."

So what was it that was buzzing in my head?

Mrs. McDonner, still far away, spoke up softly. "I believe she could have had a old blue wool cap up there. She had so many other things . . ." And she was gone again.

It took me a second more, but I finally got there. "So, if she's not lost . . . why doesn't she come home?"

16

GRAVY

If you want a smooth gravy, you've got to make a roux first. You melt butter, or actually I personally prefer heated olive oil, and add flour. It mushes up to a brown paste, then you add the already warmed liquid, slowly—and use a whisk. Don't insult the gravy with a fork or a wooden spoon. What I'm saying is, you can't add the flour later. If you do, you're doomed to lumps and a culinary disaster. I'm saying I hate lumps.

And the information I was getting now was very lumpy information indeed.

Nobody in the kitchen was answering my very interesting query. And everybody twitched a little when the front door slammed.

"Hey. It's me." It was Cedar.

I got myself craned around just in time to see him zip into the room, and I was very curious. "No wonder you didn't have to ask Mustard which abandoned farm he was talking about going to last night."

He stopped in his tracks. "Hmm?"

"Why didn't you say anything about Ms. McDonner owning that property?"

He was steady. "Is it important?"

"Right. And you don't even mention a word about her being *kin* to the little ghost girl."

He was still like a rock. "I don't take much to children's stories and idle gossip, Mr. Tucker. Or haven't you noticed yet that I'm a more or less nononsense person?"

"Oh, I've noticed. It's just normal enough to be odd in these parts."

And unexpectedly, that cracked him a smile. "Yeah. I guess that did make me a little strange in high school."

I think that might have been the first time I'd seen him smile. I pressed. "The deal is, I got to know everything. That's a fair amount of something to keep from me in this matter, wouldn't you say?"

His smile was gone. "If it seemed like Ms. McDonner or her husband had done something to make Ginny's disappearance happen, I'd say the family history would be marginally germane—but as things stand, I don't know what makes that important."

I looked back across the table. "You missed my most recent interesting question." I looked at him again. "If Ginny's not lost, why doesn't she come home, or come to you, or go some other place nice and warm? Brother Dave's church springs to mind. When you saw that she'd been up there, you knew she wasn't lost in the woods. You knew you could take Mustard back to the hospital and it didn't much matter *what* I did up there. The hat's just idle curiosity. So do you mind telling me—what's going on?"

His lips were very thin. He flashed a look at Ginny's mother, then back at me. "I believe Sydney Wicher has kidnapped Ginny."

I looked down. "I think you're jumping to conclusions."

Mr. McDonner was a more ready audience. "Damn. I shoulda known it."

I looked at their faces. They'd already made up their minds. It was looking grim for the neighbor. I had all manner of questions about Cedar and his relationship with the McDonners, but it didn't seem like the time or place. It seemed like the time or place for reason.

I raised my eyebrows. "Are we basing this new theory of yours on any evidence whatsoever?"

Cedar's voice was clear. "The state of his house, the nature of the things missing from it, and the circumstances in general."

Mrs. McDonner lowered her head along with her voice. "Plus—he's done it before."

I railed back in the chair. "Now, see—that's exactly the kind of information we were just talking about. Lumpy information." I scattered a look her way. "He's *kidnapped* her before?"

She looked at her lap. "Well . . . I mean . . . once or twice when she was out sleepwalkin' late of an evenin', and it didn't look like me nor Mr.

McDonner was anywhere close by, he's taken her in."

Mr. McDonner was less generous. "He kep' her for a day an' a half. We was out our minds lookin' for her the first time."

I sighed. I had to. "When was this? How long ago?"

Cedar answered. "Last spring—about this time of year."

Everybody nodded sagely, and I heard something strange in his voice. "Anything significant about this time of year in this regard?"

Silence. But it was a silence that was very loud indeed.

Finally it was the missus that broke. "It was just about this time of year when the Rayburn place burnt down, and Christy went missin'."

I squinted. "And Wicher often refers to your daughter as Christy, right?"

More nods.

"And you think this means he's confused enough to think Ginny is a dead little girl in need of protection from less than ideal parents."

Continued nodding.

I wasn't finished. "You think this because he also often talks to his dead wife like she's really there." I eyeballed Cedar. "Even though you told me last night you thought he was just lonely."

He shrugged.

I leaped on. "Not to mention that when you were telling us about the McDonner miscarriage you hardly batted an eye. I'd have to say that it seems to me the investigation of the incident was fairly slack."

Okay, in retrospect I kind of wish I hadn't said *that*. But that's what happens when you get riled. You blurt. That's why I try not to get riled.

No one in the room was very pleased with my little speech. Mrs. McDonner was the first to throw stones. She chunked them at Cedar; her face white and her voice choked. "You told him about *that*?"

He looked at the floor, but I could tell his face was burning. Odds were good that I could look for a whack in the schnoz from the guy—soon.

Mr. McDonner was the only calm one in the bunch. "The baby had what they call Down Syndrome . . ."

I corrected. ". . . Down's . . ."

He went on. "Uh-huh. What you call it don't mean nothin'. The plain facts is that the baby was in need of extra care and we didn't have it to give. Not to mention the way people would treat it. Children up here . . . is hard."

Mrs. McDonner was crying. Not big sobbing, but tears were there. "I didn't want to do it."

Her husband was steel. "It was my decision. She didn't have nothin' to do with it." He looked at her. "It was my fault the baby was wrong—I'm so much older'n she is."

I squinted. "Your decision?"

He nodded, very certain. "Head of the household. God gave the man dominion over the woman."

I leaned forward. "That from Brother David's pulpit?"

His face was like a fist. "I don't take much to David's church. I'm from a more . . . conservative religion."

She spoke up softly, trying to pull herself back together. "He's Temple Holiness."

Like I had any idea what that meant. "Well, far— and I mean *very* far be it from me to tell anybody else how to live, but put me down as being in general disagreement with this entire situation."

Mr. McDonner was very specific. "Don't much give a thought to *what* you have to say about it."

I hope I was just as clear. "As long as we understand one another."

Cedar finally found his voice again. "Mr. Tucker, I think we've all had just about enough of your *help*. Ginny's going to be fine. I'll find her, now that I know what's happened to her, and that'll be that. I know where Wicher goes to fish and hunt. I expect she'll be playing up there with him and everything will be normal by the end of the day. You can go on back to Atlanta now, you and your girlfriend."

I took in a good breath. "In the first place, Ms. Oglethorpe is no *girl*. And in the second place, even though we *are* friends, our relationship far surpasses your ability to understand. In the third place, I'm up here to visit with Mustard and Sissy. They asked me to help, and when I'm done helping, I'll roll on back to Atlanta. Until then I'm here."

I stood, picked up my hat from the floor and my coat from the chair. I could sense menace in the room, but no more than I was used to in plenty of situations in my daily intercourse.

The woman of the house, alone, spoke to me. "Mr. Tucker . . . thank you for . . . tryin' to help . . ." And it seemed like she had lots more to say, but the atmosphere was getting pretty thick.

I nodded. "Ma'am." I looked at Cedar. "So are you going to give me a ride back to Miss Nina's, or am I going to have to do more hiking?"

Clearly cool to the idea, and without any eye contact whatsoever, he nodded. "I'll give you a lift. Got to go back over there anyway, and I wouldn't mind getting you out of this house as soon as possible."

Without any further discussion, Cedar and I were down the hall and out the front door.

The clouds were still thick, but the air seemed softer by the minute. No more snow. In the front yard by the porch dozens of purple crocuses were popped open in the snow.

Once Officer Duffie had his Jeep cranked and we were turning around, I started up the conversation again. "You don't really think Wicher kidnapped Ginny."

"I do."

"And you think you know where he is?"

"I do."

I folded my arms in front of me. "Now, why did he do it, again? I forget."

"He . . ." But the guy was having a hard time controlling himself. "He thinks it's for her own good."

I readied myself for his response to what I had to ask. "And is it?"

Brakes. Sliding. Fist with a handful of my coat.

"Looka here, Tucker! I've had enough of this from you."

I took his little finger. It's a simple trick, really. You move quick enough, you snap it like a little twig. It comes out clean from the socket. No real damage, but it certainly incapacitates the hand it's attached to. He reared back from me.

Just in case, I also put my thumb in his esophagus, just above his sternum. His hand was on fire and he couldn't breathe. Seemed to do the trick.

I spoke calmly. "Now give me your hand, and I'll pop that finger back in its socket. It'll hurt for a while, probably swell, but it's okay in the long run." And before he could think about it, I reached over and cracked it again, only the right way this time. "You ought to get some ice for it. Can I let go of your windpipe now, or are you going to mess up my coat again?"

He really didn't have a choice. He was seconds from passing out. He nodded. I let go. He sucked in for a big breath and started coughing.

I sat back. "See, you're really not mad at me. You're mad at yourself. You're mad because you told me a secret and you really didn't want to. You're mad because I'm helping you and you think you got to do everything yourself. You're mad because Dally gets your goat and you don't know what to make of her. And you've got collective guilt in your guts about *all* these lost little girls. Now, I don't mean to come off *psychological* all over the place—but you're a *mess, boy.*"

He still couldn't breathe right. He was gasping for air. I had to take ahold of his neck and wiggle it a little, let the passage pop out into its proper shape; slammed him on the back once or twice hard. He came around.

"What . . . what the *hell* did you . . . do to me?"

"Self-defense. You'd be surprised how often a guy like me needs it."

He shook his head. "No, I wouldn't. I can't imagine you're not in trouble most of the time."

"Well, I have long periods of lying about the house when I'm fairly absent of worry."

He nodded. But he was still dizzy.

I made idle conversation. "See, I'm something of a free agent. I come when I want to, I go when I'm done. Now, it's true that I came up here for nothing more than a peep at the vistas you all keep stashed around about, and a gander at Dally's new little niece. But since I made a promise to find Ginny McDonner, I have to find her. That's how I work. I'm not at liberty to split until the promise is kept. I disagree with you about Wicher. I don't know where he is, but Ginny's out in the woods by herself. I don't know why I think that, but I do. And I've come to trust my instincts like all get out. So . . . there you have it."

He started the Jeep forward again. "You're not going to leave until Ginny's home."

"Right. I can help you, or I can work alone. I got no hard feelings, and by the way, I'm sorry I brought up the miscarriage thing. It was, trust me, an uncharacteristic bit of insensitivity on my part. Sorry." I slouched a little. "I haven't been myself, exactly, up here, for some reason. Maybe it's the thin air. I'm usually much more charming, have I mentioned that? I think I've got something like . . . well, it's the closest I'm ever going to get to feeling *parental*. I'm . . . I'm worried about the kid. Okay?"

Big sigh. "Okay." And away we went.

What would have been nearly a forty-five-minute hike for a guy like me was a five-minute drive in the Jeep, and we were parked in front of Miss Nina's again. Neither one of us got out of the car, though. I could tell he had something more to say.

"I actually *did* want your help when I picked you up here earlier, Mr. Tucker. You do have a reputation of being able to find things and people, and I want to find Ginny in the worst way—just like you do, apparently."

I smiled. "So anyway, I'd be happy to continue to lend a hand—with the official sanction of the law around here."

He looked forward, hands still on the steering wheel. "Good."

That was that. We both climbed out of the vehicle.

And what do you know, but through the big plate-glass window, who did I see dining at a corner table? None other than Fedora and the Moose.

I started to say something to Cedar, but he had his eye on Dally and David at another table. They were talking to Miss Nina and an unknown fourth—but he, the fourth, he looked a little familiar. Cedar went straight for that group.

"Mr. Hainey."

The fourth guy. He stood. Much shaking of hands.

Mr. Hainey was very sympathetic. "David here tells me you've got a missing-child situation." Then he flashed a big smile.

Cedar was very deferential. "Yes, sir, we do. But I think it's coming to a conclusion."

Hainey let his eye wander past the policeman and fall on me. "And this must be the famous Mr. Tucker."

I smiled. I swear I can be charming under the right circumstances. "They usually put the word *notorious* in front of my name."

We shook too.

He sat, went on. "Ms. Oglethorpe tells me you're helping out with this thing."

I shrugged. "Best I can."

He was happy. "Good. Good. You're the man for the job." Nice smile to Dally. "Terrible business."

She smiled back. Eyes still on Hainey, she spoke to me. "Flap, Mr. Hainey here is a field executive for BarnDoor."

I was cagey. "The home-improvement thing?"

He nodded enthusiastically.

I nodded right back. "The whole country's doing it."

So Hainey was with the evil empire of designer home improvement. He seemed like a nice enough guy. Then I remembered where I'd seen him. He was the jolly guy that was leaving Miss Nina's earlier saying good-bye to all and sundry, when I'd just awakened. I was more interested in talking with Dally about the latest developments.

"Officer Duffie believes he knows that happened to Ginny after all."

But before I could go on, Officer Duffie stopped me. "If you don't mind, Mr. Tucker, I'd prefer to keep all the information about the case confidential." Flashed a kind of official smile at Mr. Hainey. "You understand."

"Of course, of course." He was a reasonable man.

Dally skipped it, went right for the next item. "Brother David's invited us to his church."

I tried to figure out what she really wanted to do. Ordinarily Dally's church is the quiet of the sunset and the first few notes of a good tune. But she did seem kind of interested. And a guy like me loves to do a little metaphysical field research.

So I just asked her. "And are we going?"

"Sure we are."

I was unclear. "There's a service today?"

David smiled like the sun. "Service every day."

I smiled back. "Okay, then."

David stood. "Shall we?"

That took me a little off balance. "Now?"

He shot me a swell head of steam. "*Now* is all there is."

I had to smile again. "Well, you certainly got me there." I patted Cedar's arm. "By the way, the two guys I mentioned last night? The ones on the logging road? They're having breakfast at that table over there." I tilted my head in the direction of Moose and Fedora.

He didn't look, gave one nod. "Saw them when I came in. Thought that might be them." Then he looked at me. "They're kind of noticeable."

I stuck out my lower lip a little. "Like me."

"Right. I'm not going to wait for you. I'm going on up to . . . the place we discussed a moment ago."

"Without talking to those guys?" I indicated the rough set.

He looked down. "I'll have a word."

I lowered my voice. "Look. I actually hope I'm wrong—but you're not going to find Ginny up there, or Wicher either."

He made his voice softer too. "We'll see."

I looked around. "Could we make it back here and meet for lunch? Catch up?"

Big sigh. "All right. Eleven-thirty."

I nodded. "Beat the noon crowd."

Dally, David, and I started out. I caught Moose's eye.

He was very happy to see me. "Hey! It's the guy from last night."

Fedora turned around. "Well, if it ain't our fateful Indian guide, Tonto."

I tipped my own brim to him. "I think the word you're trying to say is *faithful*, and I see you found out where to get a good breakfast."

He disagreed. "Hell. They ain't got even a *dab* of corned beef hash." He looked at Moose. "How do you call it breakfast without corned beef hash?"

Moose didn't know. "Gosh. That's a good one." He thought about it.

We split. I was kind of wishing I could be a fly on the wall when Cedar met up with those two. Would have made for an amusing clash of cultures.

17

WILDFLOWERS

David had his old pickup truck out front of Miss Nina's. We climbed in, Dally in the middle. The front seat was bigger than a sofa. We actually had space in between each other.

Once we were rolling, I couldn't hold it any longer. "Officer Duffie thinks Wicher kidnapped Ginny."

Dally cracked up. "I was wondering how long you'd last in the confidential-case department."

I let her laugh. "Well, you've got to admit . . ."

She wouldn't hear of it. "I've got to admit nothing, pal. We both had an idea that Wicher was whacked."

David was very calm. "Sydney's just a lonely old man. He's not even completely in this reality. He's got one foot in another world."

Dally beat me to the obvious question. "Huh?"

He went right on driving. "That's why he talks to his dead wife. I believe he actually sees her. I believe she's actually there. Waiting just outside the normal plane."

My turn. "Waiting?"

He spoke softly. "For him to join her. Then they'll move on. They were very close. When he passes on, it'll be a happy day in many respects."

Dally was impatient with the whole premise. "Okay. Whatever. Back to Ginny."

I picked up. "Right. Ginny's out there on her own. And she *wants* to be. She's not lost at all. Get this: The McDonners own that property up where the tree house is."

She turned my way. "Get out."

"Plays up there all the time. Knows it well."

"Jesus."

David made with the stern face. "I hope that's the beginning of a prayer, Ms. Oglethorpe, and not merely an exclamation."

She turned back to him. "Just an expression. I'm very comfortable with the major figure of my culture's primary religion. We're on a first-name basis. He calls me Dally, I call him—"

I rammed in. "The point is, Ginny's not lost."

That stopped everything. Even the truck slowed down a little.

I went on. "She just doesn't want to come home, it would appear."

Dally looked out the window. "Wow." Back at me. "How come?"

"Could have something to do with *why* the McDonners own the property. They're *related* to the family that used to own it. The Little Girl of Lost Pines? Her mother was a Day."

David, bless his soul, could tell it was significant, but he didn't get it. "Why does that mean something?"

I answered. "Lot of people think that little Christy, the ghost of—"

He moved me on. "I'm familiar with that story."

"Right. Lot of people believe that her father was abusive. Maybe it runs in the family. I've read that it does."

"Isn't it about time to"—Dally nudged me—"you know . . . do the thing?"

I was embarrassed. "Yeah. I guess."

David wanted to know. "What thing?"

Dally spoke for me, even though I was kind of wishing she wouldn't. She knew I didn't really like sharing the idea with all that many people. I couldn't figure why she was so willing to spill to David.

"See, he goes into something of a trance. He kind of learned it when he was a kid. In the dream or trance or whatever it is, he sees everything. Then the thing that's missing, it's like the only missing piece of a jigsaw puzzle. All he has to do is pop that piece in, and the whole mess is clear."

David was cautious. "Remarkable. How often does it work?"

She folded her arms. "Every time."

He looked at her sideways.

She was very specific with each word. "Every single time."

I had to demur. "It's just intuition. Nothin' mysterious about it at all, really."

He looked over at me. "I don't know. Seems pretty impressive." He smiled. "Sounds like prayer."

I looked out the window. "Yeah. Well." I wanted very much to change the subject. "So where we going?"

He was agreeable. "My church." We'd turned off the main road and were going up some pretty steep dirt job. "It's on the property you were just talking about. The old Rayburn property."

Dally and I both sat forward. I got it out first. "What? Your church is on this same piece of land?"

He was serene. "That's right. The property is the whole mountain. It means nothing. Just a coincidence."

Dally sat back. "Bad choice of words."

He looked at her. "What?"

She looked straight ahead. "You have no idea how Mr. Tucker feels about coincidence."

David's church was a little like a one-room schoolhouse from what they used to call the days of yore—except it was whitewashed to beat the band. Spotless. Inside too. The joint was meticulous. The pews were rough pine boards, but they looked like they'd just been put in that morning. The altar was a pine table with what seemed to be a carved wood cross on it. There were several crates under the table.

There were no light fixtures. Didn't seem to be any electricity. The windows were plain. No stained glass. There was no pulpit. There weren't even any hymn books. The place seemed like it had just been built—wasn't even finished yet.

Dally asked. "How long you been here?"

He looked around the place with enormous affection. "Coming up on the twenty-year mark."

I looked around. "In *this* place? It looks new."

He nodded, matter-of-fact. "We like to keep it nice."

Dally glanced out the door. "Slow crowd. You're not puttin' on a show just for us, are you?"

He paid her no mind. "They'll all be here by and by."

I had my eye on the crates under the table. "What's in there?" I was afraid I knew the answer.

He looked at them. "Rattlers mostly. Some copperheads. Had water moccasins, but they don't keep as long."

Dally stared. "Snakes?"

"Uh-huh."

"In those crates?"

"Right."

"Jesus."

He was firm. "Don't start with that."

She took a step away from the altar. "Sorry."

He nodded. And with no more fuss than a step toward the wooden cross and a turn away from us, he talked to someone other than us. " 'Thus have they loved to wander . . .' Jeremiah fourteen-ten." And then he started singing.

"I am a poor wayfaring stranger
While journeying through this world of woe.
Yet there's no sickness toil nor danger
In that bright land to which I go.
I'm going there to see my Father
I'm going there, no more to roam,
I'm only going over yonder.
I'm only going over home."

And without a single drop or warning, there were people coming in the doorway. They were singing, too, taking the harmony parts. It's impossible to describe how that music sounded. It was ancient, like a minor Gregorian chant, only rougher and more emotional. No individual voice was that great, but together it sounded like—God's bellows. The Breath of Jehovah.

"I know dark clouds will gather o'er me
I know my way is rough and steep
Yet beaut'ous fields lie just before me
Where God's redeemed their vigils keep.
I'm going there to see my Father
I'm going there, no more to roam,
I'm only going over yonder.
I'm only going over home."

And in that short span of time the joint was nearly filled. I had no idea where all the people had come from. They were all ages and sizes. Nobody was dressed up. It was like they'd just put down their chores for a minute and showed up here.

David turned around, very twinkle-in-the-eye like. Shot a glance to a somewhat stunned Ms. Oglethorpe. "Wherever two or three are gathered together."

And the whole place erupted. "Praise His Name."

He nodded. "Be seated."

Everybody sat. Dally and I shoved into the group on the front row. Didn't want to miss what the master of ceremonies had already referred to as the Big Show.

He cast his eye about. His voice was low and soothing. "Today we are concerned with little Ginny McDonner . . ."

Voices here and there indicated assent.

". . . her road is long, her journey is rough . . ."

More amen-ing.

". . . 'away on a mountain, wild and bare . . .' in the words of the hymn."

His voice rose.

"Every thought in this hall must be on that little girl. Every breath in must be taken to remove the dark clouds from around her, every breath out must be made to blast her onward toward home. All else forgotten. All else forgotten."

Here and there, parishioners were rocking back and forth. Some were mumbling low. One older woman was crying. The sky started to get dark outside, and it made the place very moody. David talked on.

"Whenever any one of us is lost, lost in the land of Canaan, wild and bare, away on a mountain, delivering wildflowers to the graves of the young women, all

the wildflowers fair, rearing their lovely heads, laven-
der and crimson, low and sweet the scent of the lilacs
blooming. Faster speeding faster breaking faster
Breath of God that breaks the storm clouds like the
parting of the seas. Red seas parted, black clouds
part, the sun breaks through!"

Okay, believe it or not, there was a little ray of
light in one of the side windows. Nothing dramatic,
but some of the cloud cover was dissipating. David was hyperventilating, breathing strangely, eyes
closed, and holding up his right hand high above
his head.

"Light breaks through. Light breaks through! The
wicked serpents slide back into the deeps and the glo-
rious dove of the morning breaks into song into song
into song. Falling, tumbling billows of light spill over
the rim of heaven onto the place below and lo! Some
great miracle is at hand. Some great darkness is
bound to be obliterated bound to be blasted broken
bal do haoth. Bal do haoth!"

With no warning, a younger man two down from
Dally fell onto the floor rolling and shaking and
speaking some language that sounded familiar but
wasn't. Another man farther back stood up, both
arms straight up, and was shouting "Falling falling
falling . . ."

Then the whole place erupted. People were shouting incoherently, some from their seats, most on their
feet. Many were writhing on the floor.

A very old man, shoving himself forward in a
walker, made it to the crates under the altar table. He
threw back the lid of the one closest to him and

plunged his hand in. When he brought it back, it was filled with rattlesnakes, maybe five. He shook the hand furiously, and the snakes were twitching wildly. Then he hit himself in the face over and over again with the vipers.

Dally was pressed up against me hard enough to bust a blood vessel.

David was rocking back and forth, eyes closed tight, whispering "Following following following . . ." so that the word itself had little meaning, but the sound of the word was like a violent mantra.

The old man in the walker handed the snakes to a boy of twelve or so, and the boy touched the snakes to his arms, opened his shirt, touched the snakes to his chest.

Dally and I were inside the sound of the place: voices speaking meaningless phrases or inhuman languages, the rattling of feet and bodies on the wooden floor, the banging of crates and tables, the rattle of the snakes.

Something was happening to me that I couldn't figure. I was starting to see little flashes of light, like I was blacking out. I was getting fuzzy, my sight was obscured. Before I knew it, I was staring at the golden curtain. It was the curtain I'd always seen just before I did my little trick, and there it was, big as life. The sound went muffled, and the curtain parted, and there was a little tableau vivant, just like Robert Wilson used to make. I was in the dream state, but it was nothing like it usually was. It was very calm, where usually it was chaotic. Maybe it was a reaction to the chaos that was all around me.

The scene was very clear. It was a cartoon, like a kid's cartoon, beside a running stream. Rocky and Bullwinkle were walking on either side of Carol Anne, the little girl from the *Poltergeist* movies. They were moving away from the Wicked Witch from Oz, who was wearing a carpenter's belt. Cartoon versions of Dally and me—as children—looking only a little like Boris and Natasha from the Bullwinkle show, were swimming in the water. We were all watched over by Miss Nina, the only nonfictional character around, rocking in her rocker at the water's edge. And all around the witch dozens of ghostly figures like the lost souls in *A Christmas Carol,* were flying, swooping down on a pile of stones by the water, a pile of stones by a door in the ground. They were making loud spook noises. Those noises blended with the sounds in the church . . . and the vision dissipated like a mist. The golden curtain closed, and I was staring at the back of Dally's head. The whole thing couldn't have lasted ten seconds. The noise in the church was almost unbearable.

Then, at the height of the din, just as Dally was forced to cover her ears with her hands, David snapped upright, slammed his eyes open, stabbed his arm in the direction of one of the windows, and shouted, "There!"

Absolute silence. All heads, all bodies, all eyes spun in the direction he'd pointed. Out the window we could see a car passing the church on the dirt road. It was impossible to tell who was driving it, but it was almost certainly not Ginny McDonner.

The spell was broken. The place was still. David

was breathing hard, most of the rest were too. Dally relaxed a little. I swallowed.

One time I sat in the center of a circle of chanting monks, some guys from Tibet. I was lifted out of my body and don't try to tell me I wasn't. But I was lifted on gentle wings, in a very spiritual way. David's brief service had also given me something of the same feeling, only in a very American way: violent, drastic, and physical.

Also unacknowledged. The whole congregation, if that's what you'd call them, was moving back to sit down as if nothing whatsoever had happened.

David, still a little short of breath, smiled on all and sundry. "Thank you, friends. Ginny is so much closer to being found. The Peace that passeth understanding."

Nearly every voice: "Amen."

And that was that. Like a cyclone. The place was a little the worse for wear, but as the group got up and drifted out, everything was set aright. Inside of five minutes the place was empty again, save for we original three.

Dally let out a breath that I was pretty certain she'd been holding the whole time. "Wow." She hadn't noticed my momentary lapse into Zen Town.

David nodded. "I feel that way every time we get together."

She shook her head. "Not the way I feel, you don't. I got to admit I'm a little spooked."

He smiled. "That's part of it."

She looked at him. "Really?"

He turned and shoved the crates back under the table. "Flap? You okay?"

I looked around. I was still a little out of it. "Well, I've been to one of these things before . . ."

He turned back to us. "These things?"

I shrugged. "Snake-handling service. It was pretty much the same as this, only this was more intense."

"Where was it?"

"Rabun County."

He gave a vague gesture of dismissal. "Oh."

Yeah, that's what everybody thinks: Our stuff is the real stuff, others are just imitations.

Dally stood. "So, what was it you were pointing at? The passing car? I got news: Ginny wasn't driving."

He smiled. "No, she wasn't. Know who was?"

She shook her head. "Couldn't see."

He looked back down at the crates, making sure they were secure. "Those two men in Miss Nina's." He looked at me. "I heard you say that you saw them up here last night."

I cocked my head. "You heard that?"

He smiled bigger. "Good ears. Good eyes. Everything is clear."

I looked out the window. "So you sure it was those guys?" Moose and Fedora.

"Uh-huh."

I had a little prickly feeling. "And you think . . ."

He stopped me. "Why don't you tell me what *you* think."

My answer was that I took Dally's arm. "Well, *you're* never going to guess what just happened—so I might as well tell you. I just had a little mini-experience here."

She didn't understand. "What are you talking about?"

I looked down. "My thing, the trick—it sort of happened, just now."

"What?"

"Yeah. Not like usual. It was only a scene. No puzzle pieces, no missing link."

She looked at me good. "You do seem kind of . . . vague."

"Uh-huh."

"So what was the scene?"

I shook my head. "I got to think. I got to get a little air." I looked at David. "This was pretty weird."

He actually laughed. "Welcome to *my* world."

Dally flipped him a look. "What do those two guys in the car that just drove by here, if it *was* them— what do they have to do with anything, David?"

He shrugged. "Don't know. But I believe Flap does, somehow."

She looked me up and down. "This never happened before, a big thing out in public?"

I shook my head. "I told you, ordinarily I've got to be all by myself, surrounded by all kinds of peace and quiet."

We all started for the door.

Dally still had ahold of my arm. "So what made this happen here?"

I rubbed my eyes. "No idea."

David looked at his watch. "Want to head on back over to Miss Nina's?"

We both looked at him. Dally got to the punch line. "What for?"

He looked at me. "Don't you have a lunch date with Cedar?"

I nodded. "Yeah, but I thought I'd do that at lunchtime."

He held out his watch. "Quarter to twelve. You're late."

Dally and I looked at each other. My turn. "That can't be. We've only been here, like, ten minutes."

He shook his head. "Nearly four hours."

Dally shook *her* head. "No."

He nodded lightly. "Time compression. Happens a lot in our services. We concentrate the Universe, and the whole time thing gets messy." Held up his watch again for us to see. "Quarter to twelve."

We made it out the door, but we still didn't believe what had happened. David was very casual.

"I'm hungry."

I tried to keep up. "What's good for lunch over there?"

"I like the country-fried steak and gravy. Best gravy in the state."

I tried to concentrate on the food. "It's that good?"

He opened his truck door for me. "Miss Nina's gravy? Smooth as silk—just the way you like it."

18

STONE

The drive back to Miss Nina's was an open-window affair. The air was cold, but it was just what I needed. The other two didn't seem to mind.

Dally waited until we were down the mountain to resume her interrogation. "So what was it? What'd you see?"

I shook my head. "Nothing. It was a cartoon."

"A cartoon?"

"Like I said. Except you and I were in it too."

"Really."

I nodded. "Swimming."

"Neat."

David was just as curious. "How often do you do this . . . thing?"

I stared out the open window. "Whenever I need to."

He nodded. "And that's how you always find what you're looking for?"

"Yeah."

He sighed. "So, the Lord is leading you."

I took in a deep breath. "Well . . . I guess you could say that, from your way of thinking."

He shook his head, very innocent. "I'm not thinking."

Okay by me. "I just have a little different perspective. But it's all the same in the end, I guess."

With that he agreed. "Probably."

Dally wanted more of the dream. "What else. A cartoon of what else."

I twisted a little. "It's embarrassing."

"Why?"

"Because it's stupid."

She gave me a look. "You losing confidence in the *thing*?"

"I . . . no. It's just that this is a little out of the ordinary, okay?"

She didn't buy. "There's nothing about this that's ordinary *ever,* bud."

Good point. "Okay. I just mean I feel funny."

She shoved me. "Well, you're funny-*looking* anyway."

I nodded. "Thanks."

"So what."

"So what *what*?"

"So what was in the *dream* thingy?"

I slouched. "Okay, but you've got to not laugh."

No contract. "If it's funny, I'll laugh."

Heavy sighing on my part. "Fine. It was Rocky and Bullwinkle, okay? Happy?"

She busted—laughter everywhere. "Rocky and Bullwinkle?"

I thought about jumping out the window of the moving truck. "I used to love 'em when I was a kid, all right?"

"Yeah, well—me too, but . . ."

"There's more." Might as well tell the whole deal and get it over with. "They were walking with Carol Anne, the little girl from the *Poltergeist* movies."

More prolonged laughter. "I swear, Flap. I'm never leaving you at home for long stretches of time *ever* again. All you do is languish and watch too much television. Next time I start an out-of-town nightclub, you're going with me."

"Love to."

"And you said we were in it?"

I nodded.

She pressed. "So?"

"We were swimming in the stream, like you were reminding me of only last night."

And of all things, that shut her up. "Oh." That's all.

I thought it best at that point to leave out the Boris and Natasha part, but the rest was revealed. "And there were ghosts from, like, some scene in *A Christmas Carol,* the lost souls. They were swooping down on us like blue jays on a cat."

She leaned back. "Well, that's certainly the silliest thing I've heard in a good long while." She shook her head and mumbled, almost to herself, "Bullwinkle the Moose."

Boing, if that's the right word. Or does *duh* apply?

I shot a look so quick I think she felt it on her face. "Moose!"

She didn't get it. Why should she? She was not privy to my little nicknames for the two hoodlums from the land-acquisition division of BarnDoor.

I explained. "*Moose* is my little mental moniker for the big guy you saw eating in Miss Nina's this morning, the two guys I met last night on the logging road."

David nodded serenely. "See—they were the ones in the car that just passed by our little service." Smile. Peace that passeth understanding.

We both looked at him. Then I concentrated. "And you know how Rocky always wore that aviation hat?"

She squinted. "No, I don't know."

I shrugged. "Trust me. So the point is, my little metonymy for the other guy is *Fedora* . . ."

She was wise. ". . . on account of the chapeau he seems to be sporting."

"Bingo."

"Zowie. So they've got something to do with . . . hey, Carol Anne. The lost girl."

I had to agree. "Right. They've got something to do—" Stop the presses. If I'd been driving the truck, the brakes would have been slammed. "They took her."

"What?"

David peered over too.

I shook my head in what must have been disbelief at my own denseness. "They took Ginny. They snatched her."

"What for?" Dally frowned. "And what happened? They didn't have her when they were out by the logging road with you last night."

She had me there. "Yeah." I sat up. "But they took her . . . I think."

She shook her head. "Doesn't make sense. And where is she now, if she got away? And what's Wicher got to do with it? Anything?"

"Oh, yeah! I forgot. Get this: the Wicked Witch from *The Wizard of Oz* was flying after the little girl in the thing, the dream."

She broke out one more good-sized laugh. "You are just about as twisted as the law allows."

"Witch—Wicher."

She shoved me. "Yeah. I get it. But it's stupid."

"I know that." I appealed to David. "Isn't that what I said?"

He nodded at Dally. "I believe he did, only moments ago."

I wagged my head. "See."

She shot right back. "Don't you *see* me, Buster. This is *not* right."

"Didn't I mention something about that too, David?"

He was on my side. "You did. Or she did. One of you did."

She fussed. "All right, shut up, the both of you."

Shutting up was okay by both of us. We were pulling into Miss Nina's.

But I couldn't resist a little comment on the time-space continuum. "Man. Seems like we were just here, doesn't it?"

She scraped up a look once used to embalm dead pharaohs. "Didn't I just say *shut up*?"

Sure enough, once inside Miss Nina's it was clear David's watch was not the problem. The place was packed, and lunch was on.

There was Cedar, already eating.

I waved. He looked at his watch.

I shrugged. "We were at a church service." I shoved my head in the direction of David. "Plus, I got some ideas."

He wasn't impressed. "Really."

I nodded. "You get a chance to talk to the two out-of-towners I met last night?"

"We chatted."

"Anything?"

He looked down. "Can't tell. Didn't much care for them."

I sat down. Dally and David went on into the kitchen for lunch.

Cedar stared down at his plate. "Nothing."

"Nothing?"

"There was nothing up there. It seemed obvious when I checked that Wicher hadn't been at his little camping place for a good while."

I nodded. "Sorry." Which I genuinely was. Would have been great if the little nipper were home by now.

He started eating again. "So . . . what now?"

I lowered my voice. "I think you were right about the kidnapping now. I just think you were wrong about the perpetrator population."

That stopped him. "Say what?"

"I say that the two guys who were here earlier?

They snatched Ginny—*why* I have no idea. I'd guess business."

He was not the least bit convinced. "What in this world makes you think that?"

"Hunch." I smiled. "But I'm always right."

"So." He nodded. "I don't believe a word of this, but if you had to say, would you say they still got her?"

I shook my head. "Nope. She got away. Got to the tree hut. That's why they were wandering around loose up there last night."

"Hmm."

"And Wicher does have something to do with it. I just don't know what yet."

He shot a glance to the kitchen. "That must have been some church service."

I smiled. "It was."

David and Dally popped out of the kitchen and made it to our table. David had two plates, one in each hand. He set one down in front of me.

"You need to eat, after your experience." He smiled. It was a very fine smile indeed.

Dally set me down a giant plastic tumbler of sweet tea. "Oughta drink somethin' too." Her smile beat everything.

Cedar didn't want to, but curiosity got the better of him. "What experience?"

David hopped in. "Flap, here, hooked up with the divine. Had a vision of the spirit."

Cedar was more a man of the material world. "What?"

Dally bit into her cornbread. "He had a little

satori." She swallowed and smiled at me again. "See, I'm learning the jargon."

I had to laugh. "Right."

Cedar wasn't laughing. "Satori?"

I turned to him. "I had a little . . . insight, a small revelation about Ginny."

"What was it?"

"I just told you, Moose and Fedora took her."

"*Who* did?"

See, that's the problem with so much interior monologue. You forget that you've only been talking to yourself.

I explained. "Moose and Fedora, my little nicknames for the two goons from out of town."

Cedar rolled his eyes.

David was much more polite. "Easy to see which is which." He looked at Cedar. "Only one of them wears a hat."

He wasn't amused. "I *know* that." He stared a hole into my head. "Only a few hours earlier you were regaling me with my lack of evidence for my ideas. Now I'm supposed to go along with you based on an episode in David's church service?"

I looked at my food. "You *said* David had something for me, didn't you?"

"I did?"

Dally nodded. "Last night. Those were your exact words."

He remembered. "Oh. But I meant something a little more ordinary, like a sense of decency."

I flashed him my best look of surprise. "I'm plenty

decent." I implored Dally. "When have I ever been indecent?"

She continued working on her cornbread. "Once . . . twice tops."

I went back to Cedar. "There."

He shoved his plate away from him and stood up. "Until you have a little more for me than a *hunch*, I've got to continue investigating other avenues. Those two are a nuisance in town, hassling a lot of landowners hereabouts, but their main crime so far is their accent, far as I can tell."

I stuck out my neck. "Cedar! You kind of made a joke."

"So?"

I shook my head. "Nothing. It's just another unexpected side of you, that's all."

David intervened. "Look, Cedar. I actually think Flap has ahold of something. Could you at least hear him out, maybe wait for him to finish his lunch?"

Cedar hovered, then settled. "Since it's *you* asking, David—I will."

I lit into my vegetable plate: cut-off pan-fried corn, fried okra, black-eyed peas, and boiled collard greens. In between bites I managed a few words.

"I'd like to check up around the old Rayburn place again. I think there might be something that helps connect the two thugs with Ginny up there. Also, I'd like to look into the disappearance of Christy Rayburn. I have a strange feeling about it in light of that little altar we found up there last night."

David didn't know about that. "What altar?"

Dally wanted to tell him. "It's, like, a pile of stones with—get this—a child's *skull* on top."

He couldn't believe it. "A human skull."

She nodded. "Yeah. How 'bout that?"

"Where?"

She shrugged. "I don't know. Somewhere halfway in between the ruins of the house and the tree hut."

He looked down at his own food. "It is easy to get turned around up there. As many times as I've been hiking up there in those woods, I almost always get lost for a span. It's like you never see anything that looks familiar—then there you are, back on the road, or right by the abandoned farm, or out at the church."

I blinked. "Church. Is there a graveyard up there, by the church?"

He nodded. "That whole mountain's a grave-yard."

Ominous enough. I went on. "But there's a churchyard?"

"Yes."

"I didn't see it."

"It's on up the mountain a little farther behind the church building. In some pines."

I finished my greens. I was eating too fast. "I'd like to look up there too."

"Why?"

Dally answered. "He likes old boneyards."

David wasn't satisfied with that. "I see, but—"

I stopped him. "—But why now? Because I think it's got something to do with all this, somehow. Also"—I turned to Cedar—"now I'd like to see if we couldn't get that skull we were just talking about and run a few little tests on it."

He was irritated with that. "What for?"

I looked up. "Because I believe it may be the last remains of Christy Rayburn, the little ghost of Lost Pines."

Roughly an hour later we'd found the stone altar, and Cedar had the little skull packed, according to his perception of proper procedure, in bubble wrap and Styrofoam peanuts in a box. It seemed smaller in the daylight, like it was too small to be a ten-year-old's. But what do I know about baby skulls? Maybe it shrank.

Cedar was grave, if that's not a poor choice of words under the circumstances. "This'll be back to us in less than forty-eight hours. Then we'll know a lot more."

He didn't elaborate, but I got the impression he had something to match the skull with so that he'd know something about it. He wasn't willing to share, and I was willing, at least as far as it went for the moment, to trust him.

Dally and David volunteered to take the package back to the police station. Somebody there was going to zoom it away. I think Dally just wanted a nap. We said we'd meet back at Miss Nina's—where else?

Cedar and I were more interested in poking around there in the daylight. I kicked around in the rubble of what was left of the old place for a while, but there was really nothing there—except a powerful feeling of sadness.

Cedar took the stone altar apart, piece by piece, thinking there might be more remains underneath, but all he found was the same sort of feeling, as far as I could tell.

It wasn't any warmer, but the air didn't feel as mean as it had. The new buds and stems didn't seem that much the worse for the sudden rudeness of snow. Maybe spring would have a chance after all.

Nothing in particular impelled me toward the tree hut again, except, I guess, the same Providence that had gotten me there in the first place, the previous night. I just suddenly, after what seemed like idle wandering, found myself there.

Lots more of the climbing slats were popped off the tree. Somebody had tried to climb up after we'd left. That was clear. They'd done a good job of wrecking the ladder. I didn't see how anybody could climb it now, but I wanted to go up and see.

"Hey! Cedar? You hear me?"

It didn't exactly echo, but my voice was very crisp in the clear air.

From a good ways off: "What now?"

"Got a rope?"

"A what?"

"A rope. Somebody's been messing with the tree hut again."

I started toward the sound of his voice. He must have been doing the same with mine. We met near the top of a little ridge.

He spoke first. "Rope?"

"Somebody wrecked the ladder to the tree hut. Somebody was up there after we left last night. I want to check it out."

He looked away in the direction of the thing. "Yeah. Guess I do too."

He shot back to his Jeep for a good length of nylon rope. I played baby-sitter for the place itself. In the few minutes he was gone, a wind came up and it made the whole tree sway and creak. In that movement I thought I heard something heavy clunking around up there.

When I saw him over the ridge, I started for him. Couldn't stand still. "Come on. There's something up there."

"Like what?"

"I don't *know*. That's why I want to go up and find *out*." I practically grabbed the rope out of his hands.

We were both at the base of the tree in the next second. I was tossing the rope up to secure it over the big limb that the hut was built on—and failing fairly miserably.

Finally Cedar grabbed the rope back, fiddled with it for a second, and with one heave tossed it perfectly over and around the limb in question. He had a hold of one end while the other end fell neatly at my feet.

"Show-off."

Before he could respond, I snatched both ends again and flung myself at the trunk. I was grunting and groaning halfway up before I got to the first remaining good rung of the ladder. It held. I made the rest of my way up with relative ease.

I saw right away the *real* reason I must have been so interested in coming up there—the vision reason.

Before I was even securely settled on the big limb, I called down to Officer Duffie. "Well, this is something."

"What is it?"

"I think you'd better come up."

"What *is* it?"

I poked my head into the hut just to make sure my eyes weren't playing tricks. "It's pretty much like a dead body."

He exploded. "What?"

I poked my head back out and looked down at him. "Yeah. I'm pretty sure we got us a stiff up here." I looked at the thing again. It was kind of dark in the dimly lit, windowless playhouse. I didn't see the point in mentioning the carpenter's belt just at that moment, but it was clear who was dead in the tree hut. "Seems to be the body of Sydney Wicher."

19

DRILL

It didn't take long for Cedar to get up the trunk and onto the big limb with me, even holding his flashlight in his teeth by a loop—like a pirate. Felt kind of silly, two big old guys bent over in a tree hut—three if you counted Wicher, who was lying there wearing some sort of carpenter's belt.

Cedar commented first. "Looks like our boy here's been fixing up the place."

"It'll take even more fixing," I nodded, "if the three of us stay up here very long. I'd say we equal the weight of ten kids." I stared. "You said . . . or somebody said this place had been fixed up recently. Think Mr. Wicher was making more wooden toys for Ginny?"

He looked at the dead body. "Maybe. Can't tell if I feel like it's a kindly gesture from a lonely old man or a creepy motive from a strange one." He looked at me. "This may put a further crimp in my theory of Wicher as kidnapper."

I shrugged. "Boo Radley."

"Huh?"

"The guy's like Boo Radley—in *To Kill a Mockingbird*. A kind of spooky guardian angel."

"Maybe." He didn't sound convinced. "Anyhow . . ." And he turned on his flashlight and started looking around for something.

I looked too. "Scanning for a murder weapon?"

He gave me the sideways. "What do you think killed Mr. Wicher?"

"Could we turn him over?"

He thought about it for a second, then shined his flashlight in the hut, caught a red puddle underneath the man. "I guess that would be all right."

"Think he might have fallen on something?"

Another shrug. "Could be."

"Maybe even one of his own tools."

He sighed. "Are you saying this could just be an accident?"

"I'm saying he might have one of his tools stuck in him. How it got there, I'm *not* saying."

We rolled him over. He was a mess. He'd been lying on a Makita, a cordless, battery-operated drill. It looked like the drill bit was right in his heart. His hand was on the handle. His finger was on the trigger.

I blew out a little breath. "Takes quite a conviction to drill yourself to death."

Cedar nodded, very grimly. "Especially in the heart."

"Think anybody really expected us to believe this was a suicide?"

He looked away. "I wouldn't think so."

I sat back as best I could. "What do we do now?"

He considered. "I think we have to leave this just like it is, now. Bring back some of the boys, get prints . . . so forth."

"I guess." I made a face. "Some people believe in science. Some people believe in faith healing. Surprising as it may be, coming from an urban sophisticate such as myself, put me down on the faith-healing side."

"Meaning?"

"Meaning you play science with the boys from the lab. I have other ideas more founded in my own peculiar faith."

"Such as?"

I started down the ladder. "Such as prying into the concept that we were both wrong about Sydney here." I got a good hold of the rope and slung one leg down the side of the tree. "I think he might be a hero in this story, not a villain. I think he might even have saved Ginny McDonner's life."

"How in the world would he have done that?"

I looked up at him. "For one thing, he built this tree house, didn't he?"

"Did he?"

I was in no mood to hover. I let myself down. "You don't really think that this thing has been here for fifty years. I mean, take a look at it. Some of the wood still has the yellow Osmose sticker stapled to the end of it. And he's up here with a Makita doing repairs? Just a guess, but I think he's the architect."

He looked at the place. "I guess it's possible."

"It's not fifty years old."

He sighed big. "No. It's not. So who drilled him?"

I was on the ground. "The people who really tried to kidnap Ginny?"

"And who might that be?"

"Just guessing, once again, but I believe the culprits to be a couple of cartoon characters."

"A couple of *what*?"

I headed for the logging road. "I'm going to repeat my journey of yestereve—only in the bright light of day. I'll see you back in town."

He shouted. "Where are you going? What's that about cartoons?"

"Nothing." I didn't care about what he thought at that moment. I just cared that some little girl was now on day three in absentia and I really wanted her home with her family, such as it was. Why I wanted *that* so badly was a mystery I was willing to let be. Got no kids of my own, not likely to ever have any. Still, the parent trap, it gets you one way or the other. I was thinking that Dally's new little niece might be the closest I'd ever get to actually being a father, and I'd have to admit that's a pretty far stretch. So the feeling of helping find this lost kid . . . it was doing something to me I couldn't explain. Where do they come from, those parent juices? Why does a guy like me get them?

With all manner of thoughts of that sort, I trundled down the old log road. I made it to the place where I thought we'd found the hat. Hard to tell in the light—and to confuse me further, there were plenty of pine branches just like the one I'd cleverly used to mark the spot. But I was pretty sure I'd gotten the general area right, and started up the hill from the road, the same hill Moose and Fedora had come tumbling down the night before.

Once on top of that particular ridge, I got a little tingle of something. The ridge overlooked the cemetery behind David's church. I thought about what he'd said. The whole mountain was a graveyard. I also thought about the spooks in my dream trance—which by the way did I mention was weirder than science and I was hoping to have another crack at a more normal experience of same, if such a thing as *normal* exists in that sort of experiential realm. But I was digressing. I guess I was thinking that the experience I'd had in David's church was a teaser. A trailer, like coming attractions in the movie game. I was still waiting for the feature attraction, when I could get off to myself and really concentrate.

But as I stared down at the graveyard, all my random musing was shoved aside by a darting figure in the snow and afternoon light. It looked very much like a little girl.

"Ginny?"

I practically fell down the hill toward the vanishing phantom. By the time I was down among the tombstones, there was no motion anywhere.

I tried again. "Ginny? Don't be scared. I'm . . ."

Right. Just who exactly *was* I that a scared little kid was going to come running to? Put yourself in her place. You've already scotched a couple of kidnappers, avoided a very strange home life, and wandered around cold and hungry for a couple of days—are you really going to run into the waiting arms of some strange man swooping down from the hillside after you? Well, regardless of what anybody else would have done, *Ginny*—if that's who I'd seen—was in no mood for oddballs. She'd taken the well-known powder.

What was I going to say, anyway? "I'm a friend of the family?" Not really accurate. "I'm a policeman?" An outright fabrication. "I'm a loony from Atlanta and I had a dream about you?" Closest to the truth, and yet far from confidence-inspiring.

So in the end I opted for something *familiar*—i.e., having to do with the *family*. "Your parents sent me."

No dice. Maybe it wasn't even Ginny. Could even have been one of the kids from the church service earlier, up visiting Grandpa Walton's grave or some such. I guess it could even have been my imagination. I probably hadn't seen anything at all but a little dart of wishful thinking.

The boneyard was interesting enough. Some of the graves were old; plenty were from the Civil War. I spent a few minutes looking around, trying to calm myself and collect my thoughts—sort of hoping the phantom might return.

The church was empty. The road in front of it was vacant. The air was very still. I had the sensation that I was wandering around lost again, even though I knew right where I was.

I decided to take advantage of the situation and slip back into the church. It was quiet. Nobody was around. I thought maybe I just might be able to really break into the old subconscious vault and see what hidden treasure might be there. Who could say? Maybe there was even some residual juju left from my mini-experience, the one I'd had earlier, during David's odd service.

I took an aisle seat, settled back, and started the routine from the top, the way I'd always done it since I was a kid. Breathe in, breathe out. The sound of the breath was the only sound. The movement of the air was the only motion. The feel of the breath was the only sensation. In my mind there were miles of blank white snow. Everything was still. Everything was calm. Everything was white. White upon white upon white. I could hear the rushing of the blood, feel the breath kissing the capillaries, see the white light on the white snow from the white clouds. I was dancing with the quarks. I was elemental. I was everything.

Into such a void the images came gliding, like a glittering magic lantern show. Rocky and Bullwinkle were demonstrating how to spruce up your home with attractive vinyl siding. The house they were fixing up was in the trees and belonged to a wolf that looked familiar, but I couldn't quite place the face. Carol Anne was playing the part of Little Red Riding Hood; none other than our Miss Nina—still the only real live human being in the group—was featured as the kindly old granny. And there was Sydney Wicher, this time in the part of the woodsman who chopped up the wicked wolf. Carol Anne split the scene as he went to work. The otherworldly visitors were Casper the Friendly Ghost and his cohorts this time, not the Dickens gang, and they were gathering around the lost girl in a very protective manner. They were ushering her into a door in the ground, only it was a little like Alice going into Wonderland. They were speeding her away from the woodsman-wolf sparring match, which then got a little out of hand. First it was just a bunch of cartoon punching, but then the woodsman started using his ax and the whole act went *Grand Guignol*. Blood everywhere, and some very nasty special effects. Suddenly it was a splatter film, and I was very much not enjoying myself. At the height of the action Wicher somehow managed to cut his own head off with a chain saw. I remember thinking I was glad the little kid had gotten away and wasn't seeing all this.

Just when I was thinking that, I heard the little voice of the very kid in question. "Mister?"

I turned, and the turning snapped my head and cracked my neck and popped me right out of the trance and back to the little one-room church.

There, in the aisle beside me, was a little girl.

20

MAGIC ACT

"Mister? You okay?"

I blinked. I was afraid to move. I wasn't certain she was really there. Could have been part of the vision. Could have been—but wasn't.

"Ginny? Are you Ginny McDonner?"

She squinted at me. "Maybe I am, and maybe I'm not."

I had to smile. "Good answer. You don't know me from Adam."

She shook her head. "Sure I do. Adam's dead. You're not."

I turned ever so slightly. "Got me again. My name's Flap."

"Flap?"

"Yeah."

"Is it a nickname?"

"Naw, my parents were just that mean."

She smiled. "Uh-huh."

"So are you Ginny McDonner or not?"

"What if I am?"

"If you are, I'm very happy to meet you indeed, because I've been looking for you awhile. You're lost, you know."

"Not me."

You had to love this kid. "Yeah, but people *think* you're lost."

She squeezed her lips tight. "Maybe that's what I *want* 'em to think."

I nodded. "I see."

She gave me a very convincing once-over. "You're not from around here."

"Me? Nope. Atlanta."

"Wow."

"Uh-huh. And would you mind if I congratulate you on your diction and whatnot? You seem to be a lot more well-spoken than your parents . . . *if* you're Ginny McDonner."

"I go to school." She frowned. "They don't."

"Right."

"Plus I go on the Internet."

"You *what*?"

"I go on the Internet. They never even heard of it."

"It's what they call the generation gap. In my day it had to do with the length of somebody's hair."

"Huh?"

"Nothing. You know about computers, then."

"Duh. How you think I get on the Internet?"

"I'd guess you use computers."

She smiled again.

"Everybody's worried about you . . . *if* you're Ginny McDonner."

"I'm . . . pretty worried about myself."

I looked at her hard. "I see. You're what they call *precocious*—anybody ever accuse you of that?"

"What is it?"

"Too smart for you own good, or at least too smart for your own environment."

"I'm smart, if that's what you mean."

I shook my head. "No. I mean you seem to me to be smarter than most people your age. Actually you seem to me to be smarter than a lot of people I've met so far in Lost Pines of *any* age."

She shrugged. "I'm tops in my class."

"How old are you?"

"Ten."

"Uh-huh. What does that make you, in college already?"

Some joke. She laughed. "No. I'm in fifth. I skipped."

"You skipped a grade?"

"Yeah."

"And you're still tops in your class?"

"Yeah."

"Cool."

She looked down. "Are you with those other two men?"

I sat very still. "What other two men?"

She looked up at me. "The big man and his boss, from out of town."

"The little guy wears a hat all the time, kind of like mine?"

She nodded.

"No. I'm not with them. I'm a friend of your parents . . . if you're Ginny McDonner."

"Stop saying that."

"Okay, I will." I looked out the window. "*If* you're Ginny McDonner."

"Shut up. I'm Ginny." She was giggling.

Holy Grail. The lost child. The real little girl of Lost Pines. I sat back. "So . . . Ginny . . . how's it going?"

Another shrug. "Fine."

"Want to go home now?"

She actually jumped. "No! I can't go home now! I can't go anywhere!"

"Easy." I smiled. "Why?"

"They'd just come and get me again!"

"Who'd just come and get you again?"

"Those two men."

I nodded. "Those two we were just talking about?"

"Yes!"

"They took you away?"

She wouldn't look me in the eye. "Sort of."

I leaned forward. "What kind of *sort of*?"

"Well . . ." But she wasn't certain she wanted to share with a total stranger.

I tried prompting. "You've had a sort of adventure."

"Yeah."

I tried looking out the window too. Seemed to take the pressure off. "Let me see how much I can guess, and you tell me when I'm going wrong. Whatcha say?"

She still avoided eye contact. "I guess."

"Night before last you went sleepwalking."

Very quiet. "Yeah."

"You do that a lot?"

"Nearly every night. Doctor says it'll go away."

"Probably will. So you went sleepwalking, only this time your folks didn't come get you."

Barely audible. "They didn't."

I tried to get her to look at me. "Not their fault. They just didn't hear you."

"Mama took her pills."

I got caught in a little involuntary sighing. "Yeah, but it's still not her fault."

"I know. That man made her nervous."

"Man?"

She finally looked at me. "The other man. The happy man."

"Sorry, sugar—who's the *happy man*?"

She nodded. "He got Mama and Daddy all upset. Mama was cryin', Daddy was mad. And he was still smilin' and nice as you please."

"The 'happy man' was."

"Right."

I leaned farther forward. "You know this because . . ."

". . . I heard 'em talking loud before I went to sleep. It scared me."

"I see. What's the next thing you remember?"

"Walking on the highway with the big man and his boss."

"Being on the highway?"

She nodded. "Yeah. We went up to the picnic place."

"The Rayburn place? The abandoned farm?"

"I guess."

"Where the tree hut is?"

Big smile. "Yeah. I really like that tree hut."

I smiled back. "Me too. I been up in it."

"Have not."

"Have."

"You're too big . . ." Then she obviously thought of something. "Oh."

"What is it?"

"You must be about the same size as Mr. Wicher?"

I wanted to be really careful with that question. "Maybe."

"He's the one that built the tree hut. Built it for me and Jimmy Dendy and Hollis and Jennifer. It's our getaway."

I sat back. "And Mr. Wicher built it?"

"Yeah. We all helped. Last summer. He makes all kinds of things. He's really nice . . . for somebody so curious."

"He's *curious*, is he?"

She nodded very enthusiastically. "Quite a bit."

"*Curious* as in *strange*?"

"Right. Strange. But he's my friend and I like the little wooden family he made me." She reached into her coat pocket and produced a carved figure the size of an old-style wooden clothespin. "This is Christy."

I looked at it. "Christy . . . Rayburn?"

She looked at it like the answer might be written on it. "I guess. She's the little ghost girl."

"Uh-huh."

"She's been a big help."

"Who's been a big help?"

"Christy. She's the one that got me to the tree hut in the dark. She's the one that showed me the good hiding places. She knows them all."

"I see. She's been helping you? This little doll?"

"Sure." She turned a little. "I mean, Christy has."

"Of course you know that there are some people who would try to tell you that Christy Rayburn was just a ghost story now."

"I know that."

Silence. Creepy silence.

"Uh-huh." I leaned in toward her a little. "Well, how about this: You and I could just take a little walk down the mountain and get you back home?"

Big jump. "No!"

I tried to stand. "Wait." Damn.

She was scrambling backward. "They'll hurt Mama an' Daddy!"

"Wait." I was barely on my feet. "That won't happen."

She was scooting like she had wheels. "I can't go back now! I have to wait for the sign!"

"What sign?" I tried to nab her.

"Mr. Wicher told me not to go anywhere! He's going to leave me a sign in the tree hut. I have to go there and when it's safe for me to go home, he'll leave me a *sign*."

I froze. "You're not going to the tree house now?"

She slowed but kept retreating. "Yes, I am."

"No, sugar . . . please don't go there now . . ." But I didn't know what to tell her. That her only sign would be Wicher on ice with a drill in his ticker? Nice sign.

"Mr. Wicher helped me to get away from those two men and he *told* me to wait for the sign, just after he swooped down."

I tried to inch forward. "Mr. Wicher did what?"

"He . . ." She licked her lips, "he swooped down."

"Like on a rope or something?"

"Uh-huh."

"And it scared the two men?"

She cracked a smile. "Sure did. He made a terrible noise."

I took in a little breath. "What were you doing at the tree hut in the first place?"

"I took them there. Those men. I had to get some things."

"Things?"

"Clothes and stuff—it was cold. Plus, the tree hut, it's our little fort."

I took another step. "I see. And Wicher was waiting there for you? How'd he know?"

She looked down, then back at me. "He said he saw them take me."

Again that stopped me cold. "They . . . Wicher saw the two men take you? From where?"

"I was sleepwalking. I told you."

"Uh-huh."

"I was in the middle of the road and the two men

were about to get me and then I almost got run over
by a truck and Mr. Wicher saw the whole thing from
his front porch and then I woke up because of the
truck and then the two men were waiting on the
other side of the road and they got me."

"Jesus. That was Mustard Abernathy's truck."

"Oh." Big smile. "They had their baby yet?"

"Uh, yeah, darlin'."

"That's nice." Bigger smile.

Man. In the middle of all this she could smile
about somebody else's baby. You had to admit this
was some kind of a kid. Still didn't explain how
Wicher got to the tree hut, or what happened to him.
Didn't explain the strange timing of the events. Much
as it seemed obvious, I really hated to think of Moose
and Fedora as the type of guys that would drill somebody in the heart.

"So, Ginny . . . the two men? Were they mean to
you?"

"Oh, no. They were funny."

"Funny like you wanted to laugh or funny
strange?"

She thought again for a moment. "Both. But they
did make me laugh."

I let it go for the moment. "So you got to the tree
hut . . ."

". . . well, they were taking me to the abandoned
farm? Our picnic place."

"Right."

"And then they asked me where was the church,
and I was taking them there, only the tree hut was on

the way, and I thought I might get some better clothes there. Like I said, I was getting cold."

"I'll bet." Big flash. "By the way—did you pass by the baby skull?" Thought I might see if she knew anything about that.

"Yes." She was very solemn. "The altar."

Beat. "Right."

"You have to go by that to get to the . . . well, I mean it's the *shortest* way to the tree hut."

"Okay." Smile. "What is it, anyway?"

She was very mysterious. "It's the last remains of Christy, the Little Girl of Lost Pines."

"I see. How do you know that?"

She shrugged, and the spell of mystery was broken. "That's what the other kids say. I think it's a monkey skull."

"Really?" I cracked up. "Got a lot of monkeys up here, do you?"

She didn't find her theory as amusing as I did.

"It *could* be a monkey skull."

"Yeah. I guess it could at that. Does seem a little small for a girl your age." I started my sly encroachment once again. "Look, so Wicher, he comes swooping down . . ."

". . . Yeah."

"And what happened then?"

"Well, I went up the ladder into the hut. He started swatting at the two men with some kind of baseball bat or something. A big piece of wood, and then the two men pulled out their guns . . ."

". . . guns?"

"Uh-huh. And then Mr. Wicher, he ran away.

They ran after him. I thought they might be gone, and I almost climbed down, but Mr. Wicher ran right back and he yelled up at me. He said he'd try to get the men away from me. It was a game, he said. I was supposed to hide in the tree hut until I was certain the men had gone. And then he told me to wait for a sign—a sign at the hut." Her voice was getting faster and faster. "So then he left and I waited and waited, and after a while I heard the little man, the boss . . ."

I wanted to help calm her down. ". . . the guy in the hat . . ."

". . . right, the guy in the hat. I heard him yelling about how the *big* guy should go wait under the tree so I wouldn't get away. So I had to trick them."

"You tricked them? How?"

"When they started yelling at me, I didn't make a peep. I'm really good at being quiet. And I'm the best at hide-and-go-seek of anybody in my class."

I squinted. "So . . . what? They thought you were gone?"

Big smile. Great smile. "Uh-huh. The big guy tried to come up, but I knew he couldn't. The ladder's not strong enough for really big guys. Mr. Wicher made it that way on purpose. He said the only people that could come up were kids—and him . . . to fix the place sometimes." She whispered, "He's a small man."

"I see. Couldn't the little guy, the boss, the guy in the hat—couldn't he get up?"

She looked at me sideways with an attitude I could have deposited in any city bank. "That man? He wouldn't go up in a tree hut if his life depended on it."

"Why do you say that?" I couldn't help laughing.

"I don't say that. He did, the little guy said it for himself."

"I see."

"I was so quiet." She lowered her voice, enjoying telling me the story. "They kept yelling. Once the man in the hat, he got so mad that he fired his gun. He said he was shooting at me, but I was peeking out one of the cracks in the wall. He was shooting into the snow. After that they were sure I'd gone—they thought the guns would scare me. They thought I must have got out while they were chasing Mr. Wicher."

"You heard them say all that?"

"Yeah."

"Then what?"

She looked down. "They said a lot of bad words. The boss man did, anyway."

"I'll bet." I started my cagey move toward her one more time.

She noticed right away, and countered backward. "I'm not going home right now."

I kept moving. "Where are you going, then?"

"I told you. Tree hut."

I shook my head and tried to sound like an adult who knew what he was talking about. "There'll be people there. Policemen—Cedar Duffie, and some others."

That stopped her. "What for?"

"*I told you.* Everybody and his brother is up here looking for you. We're all worried sick."

She got me in some serious eye lock. "Well, stop worrying. I'm fine."

I nodded. "I can see that. But your parents . . ."

Still with the steady gaze. ". . . are *fine* as long as I stay *away*!"

"Maybe they are, sweetheart, but don't you *want* to come home?"

She was just at the door. She was very firm. "*Not* until I get the *sign*."

And then like something out of a slick Vegas magic act, she was gone. I mean it. I was less than ten steps from the door, and when I got to the threshold, she was nowhere to be seen. Vanished.

"*Damn* it!" Loath as I am to use profanity and whatnot, I felt this particular situation called for it. And I felt a little like Fedora, what with losing the kid and all. I'd had her right in my hands, and I'd let her get away. Some big city professional I was. What was worse, I was going to have to tell everybody about it. Dally would never let a thing like that rest.

I wandered around the yard and the surrounding area for another half hour or so, but there wasn't a trace, no footprints in the snow, no broken twigs like they tell you about in the the Scouts—nothing.

I heaved as big a sigh as I could manage, and started, once again, down the road to town, away from the church. The walk was getting monotonous, I was a bigger dope than usual, and the *real live* little girl from Lost Pines seemed to actually be the *only* one who wasn't lost at all. I'd found the Holy Grail, and I'd managed to make it vanish. I'd turned wine into water. And speaking of wine, where the *hell* was I going to get a decent glass of the stuff up in *this* neck of the woods?

21

MUSCADINE WINE

I may have mentioned once or twice that I can be something of a know-it-all when it comes to the grape. I know it's insufferable, but it is my confirmed opinion that if it does not come from France, I personally would not give you two cents for it. Take American wines, for just one example. (A) You can't make wine in a stainless-steel vat like they do a lot in these United States. You've got to use old wooden barrels. Like they do in France. (B) You can't make wine *just* for the money. It's got to be what they call an *affaire de coeur*. The maker has to be in love with the wine. It's hard for me, personally, to drink a bottle when I know the château it came from is owned by a conglomerate that also owns a Frosted Flakes factory in Battle Creek, Michigan. (C) Sulfites. These are my three arguments against American wine.

I favor, let us say, a nice Saint Emilion—I like the '86. There you have hundreds of years of tradition;

families who eat, sleep, and dream wine for generation after generation; and people who can sip one sip from a glass and tell you about the trees and the berries that grow in the region, not to mention the date, time, and temperature of the original bottling. How does that compare to a wine made by a company that also makes sugary breakfast cereal—whose advertising is "Drink our wine, it's grrrrreat?"

So I can tell you I was feeling not a little sorry for myself as I ended up on the main road and trundled my way toward downtown Lost Pines. Where was a guy like me going to get a decent glass of anything to quench my spiritual ennui? That's what a good wine does, you know: cures the soul. And I quote: "Wine that gladdens the heart." I know you hear a lot of American preachers quoting the famous "Drink thou no strong drink." But here's my answer to that: The only appropriate alcohol content for any good wine is between eleven and a half and thirteen percent. In other words, nearly *ninety* percent is *not* alcohol, so how is that strong drink, I ask you? I mean, I gave up scotch. What more do they want?

So I was playing a little game with myself as Miss Nina's came into view over the rise in the road. The rules of the game allowed as to how I could just tell Dally that I found the little nipper, she was fine, and I let her go play in the woods. We could be back at Easy before our regular dinner hour. Problem was I didn't even buy it myself.

I had no idea what time it was—later afternoon. The place was fairly empty. Dally was at a corner table gabbing with the proprietress herself. Nobody else in the joint was familiar. I zipped over to the table and sat beside Dally.

Miss Nina was going on, eyes nearly closed, rocking by the heater. "I'm closin' in on seventy. But I look older. Had a hard life." Then it seemed like she slipped off to sleep.

Dally nodded her head, even though it seemed obvious to me that the old dame didn't see it.

Then Miss Nina gave me a little lesson. "There's some coffee on back yonder, Mr. Tucker—if you want some."

Dally smiled at me. "Have a nice day at the office?"

I hesitated. She saw it.

She squinted. "What?"

I was going to have to tell her sooner or later, so what the hell. "Want to walk me to the coffee?"

She nodded. I left my coat and hat at the table.

In the kitchen we were alone. I poured. "Well . . ."

She looked at me. "Something happened."

"You could say that."

"What? Tell me."

Big sigh. I set the cup down on the counter, lowered my voice. "Keep it down, okay? I found Ginny."

Loud whisper. *"You found her?"*

"Shhh. Yeah. Or she found me, if you want to get technical. I was back in the church, David's church, trying to do my little thing, and there she was."

"Ginny?"

I rolled my eyes. "Yes, Ginny."

"You sure?"

"I said, 'Are you Ginny?' She said, 'I'm Ginny.' I mean, I didn't get a look at her driver's license, but . . ."

". . . So where is she?"

I looked at the coffee cup. "Well, see . . . that's the thing. I—she kind of got away again."

She couldn't keep her voice down at that. "*What?*"

"Shhh. Man. I knew you were going to make a big deal about this."

"Well, *yeah*."

I picked up the coffee cup. There. The worst was over. The first sentence is always the hardest. Journey of a thousand miles begins with the first step. Well begun is half done. "I got a lot of information out of her before she split."

"Why did she . . . how could you let her go?"

"I didn't *let* her. She was like *lightning,* this kid. She vanished."

"She vanished."

I sipped. "That's what I said."

She shook her head. I was pretty sure you could have defined the word *incredulous* by the look on her face. "Unbelievable."

"She was in great shape. Warm, happy . . . a little jumpy, but . . ."

"Jesus, Flap. What are you doing here drinking coffee? You go right back up there and *get* her."

I shook my head. "Not that simple. She doesn't want to be got."

"What?"

"She doesn't want to come home just now. She's waiting for a sign."

"A sign?"

I lowered my voice even more. "Yeah, but it's not going to come. She's expecting a sign from Wicher . . ."

". . . Wicher?"

"Yeah, but he's not going to give it on account of his being dead."

"Wicher's *dead*?"

"Somebody drilled him in the heart."

"He got shot? Where?"

I looked at the coffee. "In the tree hut. And he wasn't shot. He was literally drilled, like with a drill."

"In the *heart*?"

"Uh-huh."

"In the *tree hut*?"

"Um . . . right."

"Jesus."

"And that's not all."

She took my coffee and sipped some herself. "You've had quite a little afternoon."

"Yeah. Get this: Wicher built that tree hut for the kids. Wicher also saved Ginny from the *real* kidnappers—"

She interrupted. "She was really kidnapped?"

"Right. The real kidnappers were the two out-of-towners—"

"—The big guy and the guy with the hat."

"Check, but *they* lost her too."

She actually grinned. "This is some kid."

"My sentiments exactly. She's a doozy. And smart as a whip."

"So you talked to her."

I nodded. "At length. She's ten, but she's in the fifth grade. She skipped. She's on the Internet. And by the way, she thinks the ghost of Christy Rayburn is helping her find the best hiding places."

Completely ignoring the ghost part: "And why is she hiding, did she say?"

"Yeah. She thinks the mean men are going to hurt her parents if she comes home."

"Why would she think that?"

"Don't know."

Dally sighed out a healthy breath. "Anything else? See anything of Bigfoot or Elvis?"

I sipped a little more coffee. "No, but I did get a little further with my thing, my trick."

She looked at me. "And?"

"It's still not complete. It's all coming together, and it seems to be supported by the facts, however bizarre *those* might be . . . but something's missing from the process."

"Like what?"

I finished my cup. "I don't know."

She didn't know what to say—something of an unusual circumstance for our pal. "So . . . what now?"

I set the cup down. "I need to finish the thing, the trick . . . plus I need a glass of wine or two, but thanks to *you* I got none."

"Thanks to *me*?"

"Who knew this was going to be more than an afternoon excursion?"

"Not me."

I started back into the dining room. "Yeah, well—if *I'd* known, I would have brought a stash with me."

She followed. "Like you usually do."

I was irritated. "Yes. Like I usually do."

"Fine."

"Fine."

And we were in the dining room face-to-face with Mr. Hainey, the man from BarnDoor.

He smiled bigger than it looked like his face could go, and shot out his hand to shake. "Tucker! Good to see you. How goes the hunt?"

"Mixed."

He had confidence in me. "You'll get there, boy. It'll be just fine. And Ms. Oglethorpe—how are you this fine evening?"

"Swell in a hand basket."

"Good. Good. Terrible business about that old fella Wicher." He made a kind of theatrical shudder.

That stretched my neck, but I tried being coy. "What about Mr. Wicher?"

He lowered his voice. "It's okay, Mr. Tucker. It's all over town—but I understand your not wanting to talk about it." His voice was back up to a normal level. "Terrible business." He threw a smile in the direction of Miss Nina. "And how about some grub, Miss Nina!"

She didn't open her eyes. "You know where it is."

He was delighted. "Yes, I do!" Chucked a glance our way. "I *love* this place."

And he slipped gracefully into the kitchen.

Miss Nina muttered, nearly to herself, "Never trust a man that happy."

Bing. Happy. This was the *happy man.* It made too much sense for science.

Dally must have seen it on my face. "What is it, bud?"

"The happy man." I lowered my voice. "We have *got* to talk." I could barely wait to tell her what was running through my brainpan, but the happy man came back. He barely had a dab of food on his plate.

"Mr. Tucker, I understand you're something of a wine aficionado."

"I got opinions." I was itchy to get out and tell Dally my theories.

"Yes." He set his plate down at the table where my coat and hat were reposited. "You don't care much for our American wines, I understand."

"Not much."

He smiled. "Too bad. Our group owns a winery in this very region."

Dally was confused. "BarnDoor owns a château?"

He was very tickled by this notion. "That'd be something, wouldn't it? No, I mean the company that *owns* BarnDoor *also* owns the winery. Black Rock."

She inclined his way. "Pardon?"

"That's the name of the house, Black Rock wines."

"Make a lot of muscadine"—my voice was, I suppose, crammed with irony—"and, I don't know, elderberry wine, do they?"

He sat at the table. "That muscadine wine is *very* folksy. Also popular."

I shook my head. "Where? Where is it popular?"

He mistook me for someone who had an interest in the subject. "Well, Seattle, for one. They *love* that wine in Seattle. Portland. San Fran. Denver. Get the picture? They like the *folksy* quality."

"Is it actually made by folks?" My voice lilted.

Miss Nina bubbled with a little laugh.

Hainey just smiled bigger. "Yes! We hire locally. It's our policy." He turned to his food. "Although the recipe, of course, comes from corporate."

I shot Dally a look. "Of *course* the recipe comes from corporate."

"Actually that's what I'm in these here parts for." He managed to make *these here parts* sound jolly and insulting both at the same time.

Dally was droll. "What's that, exactly?"

He nibbled at a fried chicken wing. "I've got to get some land up here for the new site."

My turn. "Site?"

"For our new winery." Bite.

I nodded. "I see. Lucky you got some good help in that arena. I hear people up here are somewhat suspicious of outsiders coming to take their land."

Miss Nina chuckled again, eyes still closed.

He was undaunted. "Well, it's all in how you approach them. People are people, I've found. But I don't know what you mean about the good help. I'm up here all by myself."

I spoke evenly. "I mean the two guys you got working for you up here."

He stopped eating. He seemed genuinely baffled. "Two guys?"

Dally pitched in. "And I thought you were up here for a BarnDoor factory or whatever."

He nodded vigorously, wiping his mouth with his

paper napkin. "Oh, that too. We've had our eye on this section of the state for a while." He shifted in his chair just a little. "We want to help. This whole area has been depressed for a while. Our company will bring jobs and tourists and a good shot of money into the region. Great for everybody."

Dally cracked a little smile. "Tourists?"

He was quite serious. "Oh, yes. People love to tour wineries. That's as much of the business as the actual wine!"

I think Dally could tell I was all set to launch into my patented-wine tirade. She interceded on behalf of the happy man.

"Flap, here, only drinks French wine."

He was busy with his creamed corn. "I see. Well, a couple of the other wineries up here have done well— so I suppose we're counting on a few people who might disagree with Mr. Tucker." He turned my way and winked at me. "Plus, they've got a great golf course up there . . . where is it?" He couldn't quite remember and I was in no mood to help. "Anyway. You play golf, Mr. Tucker?"

"Me? No. Not much of a sports fan at all."

"Oh." He seemed disappointed. "Too bad. It's a great course."

I was calm. "Uh-huh. That's what *I* always look for in a great château: access to golf."

Dally saved the day. "He's just grumpy 'cause he got no sleep and he needs a drink. 'Scuse us?"

He made a little dancing gesture, half standing, nodding with his mouth full. I grabbed my coat and hat, and Dally ushered me out the door.

Before I could say anything, she was hustling me toward my car. "I was saving this for a little treat on the way home, a picnic at one of the overlooks or something, but I figure you got it coming to you now."

I was very hopeful indeed. "You brought a surprise?"

We were at the vehicle. She tapped on the passenger side. "Pop the door."

I did. She reached in the backseat and pulled out a canvas tote bag.

I tried to peer in. "What is it?"

She sighed. "It was *going* to be a surprise. But I guess I thought we'd get to it sooner than this."

She splayed open the bag and revealed the miracle at hand. Two bottles of Château La Grâce Dieu, a Saint Emilion Grand Cru, and a very fine age at that. I could barely believe my eyes.

"You can't be serious. I didn't think you could even *get* this in the States."

She shrugged. "I wouldn't know if you could or you couldn't. I had this shipped from Gironde."

I had to lean on the car. "Oh my God."

She was trying for nonchalance. "Yeah, well, don't say I never gave you anything."

"I'd *never* say that." I beamed at her. "You had this along as, what? A homeward treat?"

She looked far off down the road. "Something like that."

"Well, it would have been swell, but stern times call for desperate measures. I mean, this almost qualifies as an essential at this point, wouldn't you say?"

She was still somewhere else. "I don't know what I'd say."

I was still staring at the bottles. "This is . . . Dally?"

She finally looked at me. Hard to read what was on her face. I slowed down. "This is great—you really are somethin', you know it? So—how about we crack one open now and save the other for the drive home?"

She was still not herself. "I know how you are once you get wound up. Plus, I absolutely intend on sharin' this with you. So let's just see how it goes."

I nodded, made a decision, and took hold of her arm. "Then come with me."

I squired her into the car, handed her the canvas bag, and swung around to the driver's side. "Let's have a little picnic of our own right now."

The sun was just beginning to sink low, and the air was still plenty chilly, but the clouds were mostly gone, and the ghost of the near-full moon was evident in the eastern sky.

Dally was staring at it as we backed out into the street. "If you see the moon in the daytime, it means you'll learn some secret before bedtime."

"Huh. Never heard that one."

She was nearly inaudible. "Maybe I made it up."

We traveled the rest of the way in silence. Less than five minutes later I pulled the car into a gravel place beside David's church.

She finally spoke again. "We picnicking here?"

I nodded. "For all sorts of reasons. (A) This is where I saw Ginny. (B) I want to check out the tombstones. (C) Why not?"

She smiled. Good.

22

SMOKE

We got out of the car, and I headed for the cemetery up the hill.

She came alongside me. "So what is this you've got to talk to me about? What's this about the 'happy man'?"

I could barely hold it all in. "So get this: Ginny told me that the happy man was in her house the night she wandered off sleepwalking, and then the two men in the gangster togs snatched her and off we go, and so forth."

"What are you saying?"

I was nearly busting. "This is what I think now. I think Hainey wants to buy this land!" I spread my hands expansively to take in the whole mountain.

"Uh-huh . . ."

". . . And who owns this land? None other than the McDonners. And will they sell it? Not a bit."

She was still very fuzzy on everything. "Why not?"

"They've got so many skeletons up here you couldn't even shake a stick at them all. Guilt! That's why they don't want to sell. So let me just talk this out, okay? See, Mr. Happy gets the idea that if he snatches little Ginny and hides her out somewhere, the folks will come around to his way of thinking. And the two thugs tell me right away they're in land acquisition, so I had it in my head—and Ginny confirmed it—that they were the kidnappers. Only Ginny, God bless her, is too tough and too smart for everybody, and she manages, with the help of Mr. Wicher, to give the hoods the slip." I had a sudden jolt from my fever-dream. "Hey. Hoods. Little Red Riding Hood. What do you know."

She was completely lost by this time, so I had to explain all the images from my trance-state revelation.

She was somewhat amused. "Don't you think it's kind of cute that here you are looking for a kid and all your juju is from cartoons and fairy tales?"

"Yeah. Cute. But what keeps it from being *adorable* is the fact that somebody drilled Wicher in the old left ventricle—and somebody scared little Ginny enough to keep her from going home on account of she thinks her parents might get iced."

That got her. "Yeah. I guess the stakes are upped a little by all *that* mess."

"Right."

She was serious then. "So what do you think really accounts for the strangeness, the cartoon thing?"

I shook my head. "Got me. Maybe it *does* have

something to do with looking for a kid. I don't think I
ever looked for a missing kid before."

She tightened her lips. "Nope."

We'd arrived at the cemetery.

I started searching the stones. "So what I'm looking for now is Days and McDonners and Rayburns."

She was game. "Okay."

We searched awhile in silence, and the day began
to slip away.

Suddenly Dally made a little dancing laugh.
"Hey!"

I looked over at her, across the snow-covered
stones against the pines. What a face.

"What is it?"

She motioned. "Come here."

I did.

It seemed to be the tombstone of one Tyrus Rayburn. It was the inscription that had gotten Dally
gleeful. She read it out loud. *"Here lies Tyrus Rayburn, Burned by God's Righteousness."*

I shifted. Next to it was the grave of the missus, I
supposed. Lissa Day Rayburn. Hers held an only
sightly more cryptic message. *"Lifted to God's Right
Hand on the Smoke from the Punished Wicked."*

She looked at me. "Christy's folks. Fun couple."

"Yeah. And of course there is no grave for Christy.
That's what makes her the Little Girl of Lost Pines."

"Uh-huh."

"And don't we think that skull in the woods by the
tree hut is her last remains?"

"Do we?"

She got up beside me. "You got doubts?"

I shrugged. "Didn't the skull seem kind of small for a ten-year-old? I mean, now that I've just recently seen a ten-year-old to compare it with . . ."

She was doubtful. "Yeah, but, you don't really know anything about it."

I nodded. "Right, I'm just saying . . ."

But actually I had no idea what I was saying. I just ended it with another shrug.

Dally hoisted the bag. "What kind of ruckus would it cause if we slipped in the church to drink this? My toes are frozen."

I smiled. "What else is new?" The woman's toes could be frozen in the sand in Savannah in August at high noon.

But we skittered back down the hill nevertheless, and slipped ourselves into a back bench at the church. The place was not much warmer than outside, and it was darker, but at least our feet weren't in snow.

She produced a corkscrew, a bottle, and two thick glasses—they were cheap, but they weren't plastic. She knew how I put drinking wine out of plastic right up there with drinking American wines.

I sipped. "La Grâce Dieu. 'Grace of God'?"

"I guess. And don't get too used to it. I only ordered one case."

"What was the occasion? You don't serve this kind of stuff at your place." Easy, the South's finest nightclub, was more of a fair-scotch, good-whiskey, beers-of-many-lands kind of a place. Sure, they'd make a mixed drink if you asked, but I recalled Dally, quite late one night a few years back, staring at the vast array of bottles behind the bar—somewhat in her cups, as they say—and muttering, "One at a time, boys. One at a time."

She didn't answer my question about the wine. She had business in mind. "So tell me what you think your little vision means *this* time. It always gives me a kind of side-show shiver, whenever you talk about it."

"Thanks."

"Go on. Spill."

I sipped. "Okay."

I described both visions in detail, and let the images sink in.

She had more questions. "What were you and I doing there? Swimming? And what about the 'happy man'? Where's he? I thought that *you* thought that he was behind all this. And what the hell is Miss Nina doing there?"

"Yeah. Did I say she was the only nonfictional character in the whole deal?"

"What?"

"Yeah. She was a real live something-or-other."

She sipped. "Huh. And what about Wicher?"

I nodded. "Yeah. He's some kind of strange, wouldn't you say?"

"Not to mention some kind of dead."

"I told you not to mention that." I poured a little more into my glass. "By the way, how's Sissy and everybody?"

"Oh, yeah. Sissy's going home."

"Already?"

"They ship them out of the hospital quick these days. The entire family unit will be safe and snug at home by this evening." She glanced at her watch. "By now, actually."

I smiled. Couldn't help it. "That's great. What a family—Mustard, Sissy, and Rose."

She smiled too. "But what's in a name?"

"Yeah."

The church was nearly dark, and the wine was smoothing over quite a few of the rough edges I'd acquired in my adventures, what with climbing up a tree and seeing a dead body and finding—then losing—a cute little nipper.

"Flap?"

"Hmm?"

"You ever thought about what it'd be like to have a kid?"

"Not until just recently. Seems highly unlikely—and yet I find myself thinking just the same."

"Yeah." She settled into the corner of the pew. "Kids."

I looked over at her. With her eyes closed like that, and the expression on her face, there's not a Catholic in the nation who wouldn't have mistaken her for a saint.

I only had a second to contemplate her face. Then the silence was broken into a thousand jagged pieces by the clatter of burly men at the doorway, and the sight of firearms.

"*There* you guys are." Fedora had a tiny silver pistol of some sort.

Moose seemed completely amazed, staring at Fedora. "They're here just like you said." *His* pistol was the size of a Revolutionary War musket.

I tossed back the rest of the wine in my glass. "Boys."

Dally sat up, took in a deep breath.

I smiled at her. Maybe it was calming. "You boys haven't met my associate, Ms. Oglethorpe."

Fedora was quite taken. "This is the famous Dalliance Oglethorpe? Jeez, Ms. Oglethorpe, may I say you got the only nightclub worth spit in the entire southeastern region?"

She set down her glass. "Always happy to hear how much the joint is worth."

Fedora was not one to let notoriety deter him from his game. "So on to beeswax. You just seen little Ginny McDonner. In this very establishment, which, what is it? A church?"

I kept my eyes on him. "Good guess."

"I thought, what with the cross an' all . . ."

I sat up. "So what makes you think I saw anything of Ginny?"

He smiled. He was very polite. "You had her, then you lost her. Some detective you are."

I smiled right back. "Only following in your footsteps."

And as luck would have it, all he did was laugh. He even lowered his gun a little. "Yeah. Am I a dope or what? How'd she get away from *us?* She tell you?"

I lifted a shoulder. "Maybe she was in the tree house all along."

He spun his head around to Moose. "I *told* you she could still be up there!"

Moose seemed quite chagrined. "How *could* she be?"

Fedora was, after all was said and done, philo-sophical about the whole deal. "Don't matter, I guess. We could *never* have got up there." He smiled at Moose. "You've got to admit, if she was up there, she had to have some guts." He turned to me. "We shot off our guns a good bit to try and scare her."

"You *shot* at her?" Dally's voice was a little on the shrill side.

"No." Moose was offended. "I couldn't shoot at no kid. We shot into a snowbank."

Fedora was very kind all of a sudden. "That's right, big guy."

I tried to steer us back on course. "So what can I do for you gents, exactly? You already seem to know what a dope *I* am, and that I *got* no little kid on or about my person. So."

Fedora seemed reminded of his mission. "Right. We got to know what she told you."

Moose chimed in. "Plus, we're worried about her." He lowered his voice and thumbed at Fedora. "He won' admit it."

"Shut up."

Moose didn't shut up. "I kind of feel *responsible* for the tyke. I mean, what with us snatchin' her an' all."

Fedora spun his whole body then. "Didn't I just say shut up?"

Moose shrugged. The shoulders were the size of small cows. "Like he already don't know we're the ones that copped the kid."

Dally tried. "Now, how is it you all knew Flap had

encountered the kid in question—or that we'd be here, for that matter?"

Fedora looked back at her and just shook his head.

I kept my eye on Fedora, but I was talking to Dally. "Hainey. The happy man. He must have heard what we were saying in the kitchen. Remember, he was right outside in the dining area."

Dally nodded. "Right." She looked at Fedora. "So your boss just told you to come looking for us."

For some reason this seemed like a huge joke to both the guys.

"Yeah." Fedora was laughing. "Our boss." That's all.

I decided to break the mood. "Can't figure why it was necessary to kill Wicher, though."

That brought things to a halt.

Moose was *very* confused. "Who's Wicher?"

I locked eyes with him. "The Tarzan. The one that swooped down out of the tree house and shook you guys up so Ginny got away."

Fedora was nearly as baffled. "That's the guy's name? Wicher?"

"Uh-huh."

Fedora had his gun by his side at that point. "An' somebody popped *that* guy?"

Moose seemed almost hurt. "You think *we* did it?"

I was not convinced. "You weren't just a bit angry about the fact that he helped your little hostage get away?"

Fedora shook his head. "Sure, we was mad. You'd be too. But . . ." And I could see he was thinking fast. He sat down on the bench across the aisle from us. Then he looked over at me. "The cops think we did it?"

I nodded. "They're probably at the tree hut now. That's where he got it. They're gathering all manner of evidence against *somebody* or other, I'd imagine."

He looked at Moose. "I *told* you I had a bad feeling about all this."

Moose was nearly as upset. He was looking at the floor. "It just ain't no good snatchin' a little kid. 'Specially not one as cute as Ginny." He looked up at me with those big sad eyes. "She skipped a grade, you know. She's real smart."

I nodded. "Yeah. I know."

Dally was catching the drift. "So you guys didn't kill Wicher?"

Fedora looked down at the gun in his hand. "Lady . . . bad as this is for business, I got to tell you. I ain't never killed *nobody*."

Moose piped in, almost at the whisper, like he was telling a secret. "Me neither."

Fedora went on. "Worst I ever did was boink a guy's wife one time. He beat the crap out of me an' she got a huge divorce settlement, so I figure everything's jake on that score. An' the big guy here, I actually seen him carry a cockroach outside his apartment rather than step on it."

"They got a right t' live," Moose defended himself. "Just like everybody else."

Fedora was almost, well, imploring. "So you got to believe us. We didn't kill a soul." He looked at the floor again. "Man. This gig stinks."

Moose pocketed his pistol. He began confiding in

us, glancing at Fedora, talking to me. "He needs the
money for his sister. She gots a bum spine. Needs,
like, a motorized wheelchair. She plays th' piano."

Fedora looked up. "She's a concert pianist. Ain't
much money in it."

Moose went on. "We do dis stuff, mostly it's a
jolly-type romp, already. Da rubes don' want to sell,
we knock a scare into 'em, den dey gets alotsa money.
Everybody's happy."

Fedora waggled his head. "It's a living. Workin'
for the company."

Moose had more. "But sometimes we do what dey
call freelance—an' it usually ends up stinkin'. Dis
particular caper, for instance."

I looked hard at him. "Freelance?"

He nodded.

I wanted to make sure. "And it stinks?"

He confirmed it. "On ice—which, by the way, may
I say we got *plenty* of. An' what's the deal wit *dat*?
Dis is supposed to be da sunny South."

I shrugged. "March. What are you going to do?"

Fedora looked up. "Me? I'm going to do some
thinkin'. I don' need no cops figurin' I'm *remotely*
able to whack some local." He looked at me. "Shot?
We ain't fired these guns in a coupla years, I don't
think."

I shook my head. "Naw. Drilled."

He cocked his bean. *"How?"*

"Drilled, like with a drill. In the heart."

Moose sat down at that one. The bench creaked
underneath him.

Dally pressed. "So, the boss sent you up here?"

They looked at each other very strangely.

Dally wouldn't stop. "You thought you'd get *what* out of Flap?"

Fedora finally acquiesced. "We thought . . . maybe somethin' he knew or somethin' he said, you know, would lead us back to the kid."

Dally shoved on. "But the game is sort of up, at this point. That's more or less a dead end, a moot point. You guys botched it good."

I picked up. "The idea was simple. You cop the kid, you tell the folks they don't see her again until they sell their land." I looked around. "This land. This mountain. Your boss wants to buy this whole mountain for a tourist vineyard. And as an added bonus he gets old wood, new lumber, and all manner of yuppie home-improvement items in the bargain for another tentacle of the conglomerate. How'm I doing?"

Fedora wouldn't look me in the eye. Moose seemed more confused than ever—and that was going some.

I took this to mean I was on the beam. "But Ginny gave you the slip. So not only do you not have your ticket, you're both chumps. It's bad all the way around: for the business, for your reputations, for the boss—oh, and, by the way, it's bad for the Mc-Donners, who are going *nuts* worrying about their daughter."

Still with the silent treatment.

But Dally had a little jolt. "Hey. We ought to get to the McDonners. Tell them Ginny's okay."

I shook my head. "I thought of that. But what am I

going to say? I saw her, but she's gone again? That'll just shake their confidence in my abilities."

Dally was about to say something, when Moose interrupted. "We got to find da kid and take her home."

We all looked at him.

He went on, very firm. "It's goin' on three days, it's cold outside, and it's our fault. I made up my mind. Just now." He stood. "Let's go get 'er."

I was sympathetic, but I had to bring up the problems at hand. "Ginny thinks Wicher is going to tell her when it's safe to go home—and I think even you guys can figure out *that's* not going to happen now. By the way, did you ever tell Ginny you'd hurt her parents if something went wrong?"

They looked at each other like little kids.

Moose was wide-eyed. "No. We'd *never*."

I looked at Dally. "Do I believe this? And if I do, then who told Ginny that?"

Fedora shook his head. "You got no reason to believe us. But take a look at the big guy, here. That look like a face that could get past you in the lie department?"

He was right. I had no reason to trust them at all, but for some reason their story seemed true. I had a feeling about it, one of those funny, better-than-evidence instincts. I stared at Moose.

He stared back. "We got to." Honest to God, it looked like he was close to crying.

I looked back at Dally. "So, I got a feeling."

Dally stood too. Only moonlight was lighting the place. She seemed a little like a ghost herself. "What-

ever. I still don't trust them . . . entirely. But I agree
with Moose at least in this regard: We've got to find
Ginny. We've got to find her now."

I knew what she meant. I nodded. "There's something more to all this than I thought. Something more
than any of us knows. Ginny *really* doesn't want to
come home. I mean *bad*."

Dally looked at the Bobbsey Twins. "And if you
guys didn't put the fear into her . . ."

I looked out the window into the moonlight.
". . . There's somebody else out there after her . . .
who did."

23

MOONLIGHT

I found myself trying to figure what a picture the four of us painted stumbling around in the nighttime snow: huddled urban shadows in a Sherwood Forest. We'd decided to stick together, partly because we had not yet forged a bond of trust, and partly because we knew we were going to get lost and it's just easier to be lost in a crowd.

The sky was clear, like a polished mirror to the night, black and perfect. The moonlight was a chisel cutting into the darkness and spreading silver everywhere it could. I couldn't help thinking it looked a little like something out of *Fantasia*—which, as everyone knows, is a great movie, especially if you happen to be in any sort of an altered state or another.

The wine I'd had was just enough to keep me from minding the cold too much, and not enough to dull my appreciation of the scene. God Bless Dalliance Oglethorpe, and the Republic for which she stands.

"Shhh." Moose had heard something.

We froze. Sure enough, there were voices. Hard to tell how many, but they were hushed and conspiratorial.

I sidled up to Dally. "Which way are they? Can you tell?"

She pointed up over a little rise in between some boulders. I nodded.

The four of us got up the hill as quietly as we could, and looked down. We could see them very well: three men with rifles. No lights. They were talking, half whispering to one another.

I pulled back; gave a gander at Fedora. "Could be cops out looking for you guys."

"With hunting rifles?"

"Could it be some of *your* friends?"

He seemed insulted. "Please."

Dally peered in their direction. "Couldn't they just be out hunting?"

I looked at her. "Isn't there supposed to be some kind of season for that sort of thing?"

She shrugged. "Like I'd know."

Moose shushed us again and pointed. They were mobilizing.

I looked in the direction they were headed. "I think they may have just come from the tree hut."

Fedora's voice was squeaky. "Do we folly 'em?"

I looked at him sideways. "Folly?"

"You know . . . go after 'em."

"Ah." Quick glance to Dally. "Well, I make it a policy never to actually go *after* guys with guns. They come after *me* sometimes, but never the other way around."

Moose nodded his big old head. "Good thinkin'."

The rifle trio slowly vanished through the trees. I straightened up. "Well, Cedar Duffie, the constable hereabouts, said he was callin' the boys from the lab to get a peep at Wicher. Maybe he's got some sort of posse out." I looked at Dally. "Or maybe they really are just hunters."

Dally had apparently decided to have a little fun at the expense of our boys. "Or they could be some god-awful militia group. There's a lot of that up here. They could be working on their own—out to get you guys. Man." She shook her head. "I sure wouldn't want to be in their hands. Most of them are, like, neo-Nazis and they've *really* got a way with a prisoner."

Fedora looked over at Moose, his eyes very wide open. "Jeez, man. What if it's *them*? We got to get out of here."

Dally wouldn't let up. "Ever squeal like a pig?"

Couldn't help it. Couldn't keep a straight face. I busted out laughing.

Fedora relaxed—slightly. "Oh. Oh. I see. You think you're funny." Shot a look at Moose. "I *hate* this place! I want to go home."

Moose was stoically calm. "We're going to find Ginny." That's all.

I looked at him. His face was serene in the moonlight. That's what comes of knowing what to do. See, the only *real* problem in life, as I like to point out every chance I get, is ambivalence. That's right. Once you've decided what to do, and you really mean it, there's no problem. You just do it. That's why all your finer existential thinkers will tell you to go ahead and make a decision—any decision—and *commit* to it. They'd also like to tell you there's no such thing as wrong or right, there's *only* action. Action is the solution to any problem—and any action will do. Me? I'm not so convinced of that part. I'd agree that right and wrong has a lot to do with interpretation of phenomena, but then there's the Taoist in me that would have me believe there was also such a thing as the right path. Plus the Buddhist in me would have a word or two to say about right action, right motive, right speech, and so forth. But I digress. I was only thinking at that moment that Moose had found his heart, and was about to follow it with a good dose of action. Which made him, in that particular instance, the man to admire.

And in that moment of reflection I had a small occurrence. It wasn't a shock wave, it wasn't an avalanche—like it sometimes is. A piece of the puzzle just drifted into place, like a single snowflake dancing down after the storm was over. I saw something, clear as moonlight, that made sense. I had an answer.

I smiled over at Moose. "Okay, pal. Let's go get her."

He turned slowly in my direction. "You know where she is?"

I looked at Dally. "Well, as a matter of fact, I do have an idea."

She squinted. "Something in the thing, the dream?"

"Yeah."

"Such as?"

I looked out across the snow. "You know how—in the thing—there were, both times—ghosts?"

She nodded. "Casper the Friendly, and . . . what else?"

"Dickens."

"Huh?"

"The lost souls from *Christmas Carol*."

She remembered. "Oh, yeah." She cocked her head. "What about that?"

I smiled. "Both times they were leading the Little Lost Girl to a door in the ground."

She was still trying to focus on the memory of what I'd told her about the trance thing. "Yeah . . . I sort of remember that." She looked at me. "Kind of a Dali image, door in the ground. I just kind of thought it was, you know, one of those dream images that don't—"

I finished. "—quite make sense. Me too. Until just now."

"What's different now?"

"Satori. I've had a minor revelation."

"Oh, really. We got time for that?" She looked at the two boys, very droll. "Stand back, he's had a minor revelation."

They were both looking at me like I was on fire. Maybe I had a funny look on my face. I get that sometimes, with a satori.

She nudged. "So it's *not* a Dali image, this door in the ground?"

I shook my head and started out in the direction of the abandoned farm. "Nope. It's a storm cellar."

We were nearly to the site of the old Rayburn place before I felt like talking again. The others were following, Dally was right by my side.

I turned to her. "This is, see, a textbook example of how this thing works."

Her eyelids were heavy. "Are you writing a *textbook* on the subject?"

I ignored. "I must have seen a storm-cellar door in the ruins, but I wasn't completely *conscious* of it. That's what the dream-thing does, it points out what I know but I don't know I know."

The moon was all over the joint, what with the snow reflecting and the night so clear. Looked like stage lighting.

Everybody was looking at me, under the impression I had some perfect idea about what to do next. Not entirely willing to disappoint, I hauled myself down to the site of the Rayburn-family conflagration.

Now, what determines whether it's late winter or early spring, you'd imagine, is largely a matter of perception and interpretation, as I had been reflecting on only moments before. But most would agree that snow on the ground and the general brooding ambience of the scene made it late in the winter, when the year is just about as old as it's going to get, weather-wise; life-cycle speaking.

I stood in the ancient ashes and rubble, lightly kicking at the snow and the wood, wandering more or less aimlessly, which is the only way to wander, let me tell you.

Then there it was—a door in the ground. I could only see the faintest outline—but it was there all right.

I motioned the others over. I wanted witnesses for the unveiling, the resurrection, the rolling back of the stone.

As I grabbed the handle and started to pull, I could hear little noises from inside.

The door pulled back, and it flopped on the ground, revealing the stairway down to the storm cellar. There was a faint odor of burning oil. Somebody'd just blown out an oil lamp. I knelt down.

"Hey, Ginny. Remember me? The guy with the funny name? Flap?"

A little rustle, almost like a mouse.

"I've got Sissy's cousin up here with me. Want to meet her?"

All of a sudden I realized that also beside me were the two guys on earth she was most afraid of, and maybe with good cause. I gave them a look like a bazooka, and they backed up quick. Dally moved in so maybe the little kid could see what Sissy's cousin looked like.

Beat. Silver silence. Silver snow. Silver moonlight.

Then a wee voice from down in the darkness. "You're Sissy's cousin?"

Dally smiled. "Yup. And I take it you're Ginny McDonner. We been looking for you."

Ginny, the new lost little girl, moved into a small

spot of moonlight. "I've been here all the time." Like it ought to have been obvious.

Dally nodded. "You're just smarter than most."

The kid shot a look my direction. "That's what he said."

"He was right."

She just shrugged.

I looked down at her. "Coming up?"

"Who else is up there with you?"

I saw absolutely no point in messing with the tyke any further. "Those two guys. The two mean men who nipped you on the side of the road the other night. They're here. But you've got to believe me, they're just as worried about you as we are."

She shrugged. "I know. They were nice, I guess. The big guy's dumb as a brick, but it was like being with another kid, sort of."

"Yeah." I looked over at Moose. "I know what you mean."

"So, is the game over?"

I took a gander at Dally.

She answered. "That's right, sugar. We got the sign. It's okay to come home now."

She was skeptical. "Mr. Wicher gave *you* the sign?"

I jumped in. "Uh, no . . . we just happened to see it . . . in the tree hut."

She nodded. "Oh." She started up the ladder. Then she stopped. "Hey, wait—I was just over there a while ago, and it wasn't there." She locked me in a very suspicious gaze indeed. "What *was* the sign?"

Now, this was one of those moments when you

just had to go skating. If the ice was too thin, you dropped, you froze, you were gone. On the other hand, if you were slick enough, light enough, fast enough, you got to the other side. So, I skated. Didn't even really think. I just blurted. Sometimes blurting is good.

"It was a cartoon."

She sighed. "Okay." And she started up the ladder again.

Dally gave me a look she usually reserved for expensive meals and gifts.

I nodded. Sometimes the magic works. Really. Not to mention that the entire tree hut had practically been papered with cartoons and kids' drawings. I mean, I was good—but ultimately it was just a clever parlor trick.

I caught hold of Ginny's arm to help her out the last few steps. "There you go, sugar."

She got her bearings, then nodded at Moose and Fedora. "Hey."

You wouldn't have thought it possible for a guy like Moose to have what they call a beatific look, but he did. Fedora was by no means a piker in the adoration department either.

Moose's eyes were glistening. "We was so *worried* about yous."

She was a kid. "I was *fine*." She looked at me with a withering, long-suffering number. "Honestly." Big shaking of the head.

I peered down in the storm cellar. "Nice hiding place."

"Uh-huh."

Dally looked in too. "Well stocked."

Ginny nodded. "Yeah. Christy put all that stuff there."

"Really?" I looked at Dally.

Dally blew out a little breath. "Christy—the Lost Girl?"

I sort of leaned over Ginny. "We talked about this, right? Christy hasn't been around for, like, fifty years. And most of that stuff down there looks new. I don't think they had, for example, Coke in cans that far back."

Ginny reached into her pocket and pulled out the little wooden doll, the one she'd showed me before. She held it out to us. "No. I mean, this Christy told me."

Dally wouldn't take it. "How?"

Ginny lowered the doll a little, like she was tired of playing a game. "Well, it was Mr. Wicher, really. He made the doll, you know, and he'd put it up to his ear and . . . I mean, it was all a sort of a joke, but, then, when everything that happened was like the doll said . . . I didn't know what to think."

"Mr. Wicher put the doll to his ear, and the doll told him what to do?" Dally asked.

She nodded. "Yeah."

Dally and I exchanged a look.

Ginny went on. "That's how we knew the storm cellar was here." She lowered her voice. "That's how I knew my parents might get hurt."

I looked at Dally hard, and whispered, "So this makes Wicher . . . ?"

She nodded, whispering back. ". . . nuts? In on some bad deal? The weirdest guy in town?"

I shrugged. "All three?"

Moose couldn't hold back anymore. "Hey, sweetie."

She smiled. "Hi."

He lowered his head. "You know we din't hurt your folks. We would *never*."

She didn't know for sure. "Well . . ."

He insisted. "And we didn't have nothin' to do wit that guy gettin' drilled . . ."

But Dally quickly intervened, pulling at her coat. "Are you warm enough, sweetheart? Are you hungry?"

She nodded, looked around at all of us. Then she wrinkled her forehead. "Could I finally . . . just go home now?"

24

LIGHTNING

Before anybody could answer, there was a low thunder in the bushes at the edge of the wood where the road was, and the hunting party emerged brandishing all manner of rifles. Their voices were still hushed.

"Hey, they *did* find 'er!"

"There she is."

"Hey, Ginny. Come over here, darlin'."

Ginny sidled up right against me, for some reason. Before I knew what was happening, she'd slipped her little hand in mine and tried to hide behind me. Ever held a little kid's hand in yours? Quite the feeling. Suddenly the storm cellar wasn't a sepulcher at all. It was a cave, and I was feeling some sort of primal parental thing all over me.

I spoke very clearly. "You just stay right here, sugar."

Dally flanked me and we both stared at the posse. Then Moose made his move. He smeared his gun out of his jacket like he was wiping water from a window and leveled it at the group.

Fedora was more subtle. He removed his pistol from the holster like he was going to pay for dinner— held out his little silver weapon like a credit card.

And of all people, Moose cast himself in the role of spokes-model. "Let's all just behave. You don' want to shoot me, and I don' want to get shot. The tyke stays wit us. Yous vamoose."

Silence.

I was pretty sure the boys hadn't understood a word Moose had said. I was about to translate when lightning erupted from the rifles, and bullets sliced up the night.

I tossed Ginny and Dalliance into the snow and made for what was left of the old chimney, the only cover close to me.

I looked back at Dally. "Tree hut!"

She and the kid were up and running toward the woods away from the rifle gang before I had the *t* in *hut* out of my mouth.

The shooting was ripping up the air.

I slipped a half brick out of the chimney rubble and hefted it. I used to chuck rocks at rats in the county dump back home when I was a kid. I could snap one at fifty paces.

I heaved my brick through the air and it beaned one guy good. He went down. The others set off more gunfire and beat it into the relative cover of the bushes whence they'd come.

I looked over at my boys. Moose was down. There was blood.

Fedora was calling out to me. "Hey, pal! Give me a hand, will you?"

I looked at the woods. "Okay."

He emptied his pistol in the direction of the hunters. In the moment it took before they could fire back, I had made it to our fallen hero.

Moose was smiling. "I been shot lots worse'n dis." Then the smile took an exit. "But now I got to eat that crummy hospital food again."

I nodded. "Tell you what. You get yourself to the hospital, and I'll get to Miss Nina's and pick you up some decent grub."

Fedora made a face. "That slop?"

Moose closed his eyes. "I like it. What's that crunchy stuff that tastes like popcorn?"

I took a guess. "Fried okra. It's battered in cornmeal and salt."

He nodded, eyes still closed. "It's good."

Fedora was gauging distances. "Think we could get him to the church? We got our car there."

I only had to think about it for a second. "We can't drag him all the way to the church. Not with those guys shooting at us."

He peered into the shadows where they were hiding. "Yeah. Guess not." Then he took Moose's gun out of the big guy's hand and leveled it at the riflemen with a very ominous look of resignation. "Well, then."

And he opened fire. The thing sounded like a battleship.

The rifles answered right away.

Then, just like you sometimes see in the movies, a

bullet zipped right by us, knocking off Fedora's fedora. *Now* what was I going to call him?

I was having a quick review of the highlights in the
events of my life, what with the bullets zipping all
about my ears, when something slogged around in
the back of my subconscious just enough to pop up to
the surface for one second. It was a simple question:
What was Miss Nina doing in my dream-thing, and
why was she the only real person in it?

Before I could get any farther in my thinking, a
truly heroic form burst onto the scene. In the best
tradition of the Lone Ranger and the last-minute rescue, Officer Cedar Duffie suddenly flew into the
chaos, hollering, shooting off a signal flare in each
hand, and kicking up snow like it was shattered glass.

"What the *hell* is going on here?"

Even the night air seemed shocked into silence. In
the sudden quiet I saw, just behind him, Dalliance
and Ginny. They were standing side by side at the
edge of what must have been, a long time ago, the
beginning of the yard of the old Rayburn farm.

He looked in the direction of the bushes. "You
boys get out here, *now!*"

They stumbled into the open, muttering:

"They started it."

"Hey, Cedar."

"Look: Ginny! Hey, Ginny."

They smiled and waved at the kid. She dodged behind Dally.

Cedar was more interested in my direction.
"Who's down?"

I stood up. "The big guy. Your boys shot him."

"How bad?"

"Needs an ambulance now, if you ask me."

Cedar unhooked something from his belt, talked into it, then snapped it back.

"On the way. Now let's talk about how you knew where Ginny was hiding." He took a step in my direction. "And what you're doing here with her kidnappers."

I was steady. "Yeah, they nabbed the kid, but they lost her again right away. There was somebody *else* keeping her from going home. These guys, they were just lost."

"Somebody *else*?"

I nodded. "Wicher."

He actually laughed. He was having quite a night, what with cursing and laughing all within the same five minutes. "Wicher? We already dispensed with that idea, remember?"

I smiled big. "Yeah. But he was a second stringer, after the out-of-towners. See, this way, you an' me, we *both* get to be right." I looked down at Moose and fedoraless Fedora. "And by the way, I don't think these two had anything to do with what's happened to Wicher either."

Cedar looked down at the snow. "Well, I found some more information in his house that seems pretty strange in that regard."

"Like what?"

He glanced over at Ginny, then shook his head. I understood.

He went on. "Plus, we already got the results back from the lab about the other item"—then another glance in the kid's direction—"at the stone-altar place."

He was talking about the skull. "Oh?"

He nodded. "It's absolutely *not* Christy Rayburn."

I looked at Ginny. "Wouldn't be a monkey skull, would it?"

She opened her mouth. She got it. I could see the look on her face. She looked at the cop.

He squinted at me. "Monkey skull. Where would you get an idea like that?"

I looked down. "Could be a monkey skull."

He was confused. "It's not."

"What is it, then?"

He shuffled a little. "I'd rather not say just at the moment." He looked around. "I believe we have quite a bit to discuss."

I agreed. "Right. For example, I'm telling you we still don't know who's behind the kidnapping exactly. I think that Hainey guy, from BarnDoor—he's got something to do with it."

"Hainey?" Cedar raised his eyebrows. "I guess that could be."

I smiled at Ginny, then looked down at Moose. "Why don't we get our big boy, here, over to the hospital, and the rest of us take Ginny over to Miss Nina's for some hot food. She's hungry. What time is it?"

He glanced at his watch and smiled. "I believe we can just make it."

Dally looked down at the kid. "How about that, hon? We'll call and have your folks meet us there. It'll be a big night out."

She grinned. "Okay."

Dally looked at Cedar. "Call the McDonners?"

He nodded. "Sure."

From my feet the weakening voice of the Moose rose up from where he lay in the moonlight. "Don't forget my fried whatsits."

Fedora looked over at Cedar. "Let me go with him to the hospital, okay?"

Cedar hesitated.

Fedora insisted. "You can have the rifle boys, there, stand guard on me if you want. I just got to go with him, you get me?"

I had to ask, looking over at the hunting party. "Are they *really* your deputies?"

He nodded, disgusted. "Uh-huh."

I looked back at Cedar. "They fired first, you know."

He avoided my look, glanced over at them instead. "I know. I was just over by the tree hut. I heard the rifles . . . first."

The deputies all tried looking elsewhere.

Cedar took charge. "Okay, Jeff. You and Deacon go with our prisoners. They *both* stay at the hospital until I get there. And they *both* stay very healthy. Do you all understand me?"

One of them answered. "Yes, sir."

Another one shifted his weight. "Um, Cedar? Sorry 'bout the . . . I mean . . . they did *draw* on us."

He looked at me. "And they are the kidnappers."

I shrugged. "Why don't you reserve judgment until you've heard it all."

He nodded slowly. "Okay." Then he leveled a very official countenance. "There's something you're not telling me, isn't there?"

I agreed. "Plenty. I haven't had a chance to completely put it all together, but I'm just now beginning to gather one strange theory. I'm certain you'll find it amusing."

He tilted his head at me. "Just *now*?"

"I get very philosophical when I get that close to dying. Your boys were shootin' at me real good."

Then Fedora looked up at me and whispered, "Pal? You got the wrong idea about who our boss is, you know."

Before I could launch into further questioning concerning *that* particular subject, the little voice of Ginny McDonner interrupted.

She was holding up the wooden doll again. This time to her own ear. She was nodding and looking up at Dally. "Christy say's she's hungry too. And she wants to hear Flap's story. Can we go now?"

I started adding up the past couple of days for the nipper. She'd been sleepwalking, kidnapped, chased, hidden in a tree hut and a storm cellar, cold, hungry, worried about her own life and the lives of her parents, and then, for dessert, witnessed a shoot-out. I figured it was enough to justify a talking doll.

Dally smiled down at the kid, obviously having done more or less the same figuring that I had. "She wants to hear the story, huh? Flap's pretty good at telling this kind of story."

Then Ginny McDonner looked over right into my eyes with a very adult, exceedingly serious gaze. "Oh, she already knows this story. She just wants to make sure he tells it right."

Creepy.

Dally petted Ginny's head. "You're just tired, sweetheart."

Ginny's unearthly eyes were still locked onto me. "Uh-huh, but I'm not nearly as tired as Christy. She's been out here a *lot* longer than I have."

25

CHRISTY

Most everybody had gone from Miss Nina's by the time our little troupe arrived at the eatery. Miss Nina herself was asleep, or seemed to be, in the rocker by the heater. One or two tables were just finishing the last of the banana pudding.

Dally and the young Ms. McDonner headed right for the kitchen. Cedar had a word with the folks at the other tables, and there was a bluster of commotion as they angled out the door.

Then the policeman headed for Miss Nina.

I stopped him. "What are you doing?"

He seemed surprised. "I'm going to send her to bed. She needs her rest and we need a little privacy."

I looked over at our comatose hostess. "Yeah. Well, the fact is—Miss Nina needs to stick around. She's a player."

That shook him up. "What in this *world* are you talking about?"

I nodded in her direction. "Miss Nina?"

Eyes still closed, and without a visible motion, she answered, "Mr. Tucker."

"Got a minute?"

That opened her eyes. "What for?"

I raised my eyebrows. "It's story time."

She nodded slowly. "I see. And you figure you got a story worth my hearin'?"

I looked at her profile. "No, ma'am. All I've actually got is an *idea*. The story—that'll kind of emerge as we all discuss it."

She leaned forward a little. "That how it's done?"

"How *what's* done?"

She leveled what you'd have to call a spry look at me. "You found Ginny."

I nodded. "Had some help."

She tried, and failed, to stand. "You think you know what happened."

"Like I said, I've just got some ideas."

She sat back. "Well, would you mind havin' your little meetin' over this way? I seem to be a bit reduced."

Ginny came back in, waving a plate piled with enough food for a lumberjack. "Fried chicken!"

I nodded. "No country-fried steak?"

She twitched her head in the direction of the kitchen. "She's got it."

On cue, Dally came in with another plate, just as packed, and sure enough starring country-fried steak.

I motioned them over to the table by the heater. When the five of us were seated comfortably, and the kid was chowing down to beat the band, I felt it was time to begin.

"I feel this is a story about commerce. Man comes to town. Man wants to buy land. Locals don't want to sell. There's a special plum, a whole mountain, just right for the man's enterprise, but the family won't even talk to him about selling it. It's not a question of money. They have secrets and family and all manner of skeletons buried up there. Nothing in this world could make them part with it. So the man hires some out-of-town goons to kidnap the cute little daughter of the family. Family gets the kid back if they sell the land. It's that simple. Only the goons lose the kid right away because she's smarter than any other *twenty* kids, and way smarter than the two goons in question."

Mouth full, staring at her food, Ginny still managed a commentary. "*That* didn't take much."

I went on. "Even though her folks didn't see the kidnapping, the next-door neighbor *did*. He decided to come to the rescue. He hid out in the tree house he'd made for the kids, hoping, or almost knowing for certain, that Ginny will take them there because it was their getaway, their hideout."

Ginny sipped her sweet tea. "Easy. They didn't want me to freeze to death. They weren't *evil*."

I had to smile. "Right. Not evil, just stupid. So the neighbor in question, Wicher, swoops down like Tarzan, frightens our somewhat impressionable kidnappers. They scatter. Wicher and Ginny cook up a quick scheme, and *poof*, the whole abduction scenario is foiled but good."

Cedar joined in the fun. "There. So why didn't Ginny just come home then?"

I nodded, very sagelike. "Right. She didn't because Wicher told her it wasn't safe. He told her the goons would hurt her family."

Ginny finally looked up from her food. "I'm always worried about Mama. She's . . . a nervous person."

Cedar looked down. Nothing to say.

I looked at Ginny. "Ginny McDonner is the queen of hide-and-seek. She excels. Nobody can find her. But she's got help. She's got a magic doll."

Cedar looked up again. "A *what*?"

"Wicher gets secret messages from the little Christy Rayburn doll he carved for Ginny."

Dally couldn't resist any longer. "Making him the king of the nuts."

I saw a little something, couldn't tell what, in the way Miss Nina shifted in her rocker.

I tapped on the table a little. "Yeah, Wicher was a little lose in the hat rack, but he had to be in on some kind of bad deal. What other reason would there be for telling Ginny not to go home?"

Cedar wasn't convinced. "Unless the hired guns actually *were* threatening the McDonners."

I looked at him. "Did *they* ever tell you that?"

He shrugged. "The McDonners? No."

I looked back at the kid. "The fact is, Ginny got away so quick, the goons didn't even have time to call the McDonners or write 'em or whatever they were going to do to make their demands. It all went south too fast."

Cedar talked slow. "So you're saying . . . somebody else had a deal or was in on the deal or had some reason to keep Ginny from going home."

I nodded. "That's what I'm saying."

"For the land up there, the Rayburn place, Black Pine Mountain."

"Right."

He shook his head. "For a home-improvement factory?"

I squinted. "Worse. For an American winery. Much more evil."

He just stared.

Dally came to the rescue. "Hainey told us he wants the mountain for a touristy château. Great for the local economy."

He sat back. "Kidnap a little girl and terrify a family just for a tourist attraction?"

I shook my head. "No. For money. The kidnapping thing, it not only makes the owners of the property more liable to sell but it brings the price of the land way down, I'd imagine."

He got sterner. "And this is all *Hainey*?"

I tapped again. "I thought so. But the boys insist that he's *not* their boss after all."

He stared at his hands. "The boys? You mean the kidnappers?"

"Uh-huh."

"And why would you believe them?"

I tilted my head a little. "I don't know. I just do."

Ginny yawned so loud it made us all laugh.

She looked around the table, smiling herself. "I

guess I might be a little sleepy." She peeped at Cedar. "Where's Mama an' Daddy?"

He smiled at her. "On their way, darlin'."   .

She stared over at a booth, then back at Miss Nina. "Can I go over there an' lie down?"

Miss Nina was the only one avoiding looking at the kid. She just shrugged. "Suit yourself."

Ginny dragged over to the booth, threw her little self down, and was breathing steadily before her head hit the seat.

I returned my attention to the adults. "So here's where it gets really dark: I believe none other than our Miss Nina was the inside contact for the job."

Silence all around.

Finally Nina herself chuckled, or maybe cackled, a little. "You got no idea what's goin' on."

I pressed. "Oh, really? How does a guy like Hainey figure the psychology of the McDonners? I mean he can find out who owns the land he wants by just researching the deeds or whatnot, but how does he know that hassling them will make the missus take her pills? How does he know the little girl's a sleep-walker? Two essential bits of knowledge for the ab-duction scenario. And who sits in this very joint every day and listens to everything everybody says about everything? None other than the proprietress. And she's got a system, to boot. She seems to be asleep, only she actually sees and hears everything." I stabbed her with a look. "You were in on the deal with Hainey for a slice of the dough."

She laughed again, and countered my stabbing

gaze with an overdose of some hideous folk poison. "I said you got no *idea* what's goin' on. None."

I turned to Cedar. "Any particular relationship between Wicher and Miss Nina that you know of?"

"No." Then he sat up. "Not that I *know* of."

I tried a stalling tactic, hoping that it might loosen Miss Nina's resolve. I asked Cedar a key question. "And what's the news you said you found out about Wicher? Something in his house you said was strange."

Cedar sat forward. "Right. It was a newspaper headline."

Dally caught that one. "Newspaper?"

He shrugged. "Tabloid. Supermarket deal."

"What was the headline?"

He quoted. "FLORIDA MAN IN BIZARRE SUICIDE. All caps."

She took in a breath. "How bizarre."

Cedar took a quick glance at Ginny, to make sure she was asleep. "Drilled nineteen holes in his skull with a power drill."

That altered the atmosphere in the place, as anyone might imagine. I had to ask. "*Nineteen* holes? Like, the first *eighteen* didn't do the trick?"

He shook his head. "All they could figure is that the first one severed some nerve and he didn't feel anything anymore."

Dally sat back. "Yeah, but . . ."

Cedar moved on. "Anyway, that's started some of us to thinking Wicher might be a suicide after all."

And, brother, did *that* sentence get a reaction from our Miss Nina. She sat bolt upright and twisted with a lightning speed I wouldn't have imagined her capable of. "Sydney?"

Cedar didn't understand. "Sydney Wicher's dead."

"Dead?"

He nodded. "We think he might have killed himself, but the circumstances are so strange—"

I interrupted. "Is this what the so-called boys in the lab came up with?"

He looked at me. "No other fingerprints. No evidence that anybody was up there with him. And then . . . the newspaper . . . I don't really know what to think."

Miss Nina's entire countenance had altered significantly. "Sydney's dead."

I could tell Dally had noticed something in her voice too.

She spoke very softly to Miss Nina. "You knew him well? You were friends?"

She just stared out the window, but there was a movie, a very long movie, playing out behind her eyes.

Before we could even get a gander at the credits, the front door of the restaurant burst open and Mrs. McDonner came flying in.

"Where is she?"

Ginny was startled and sat up. "Mama?"

Mrs. McDonner made it to the kid in a single jump, it seemed like. They were hugging each other so close, it was impossible to tell where one left off and the other started up.

Mr. McDonner was slower coming in, but no less enthusiastic about the situation. He was clutching the other two but good inside of three seconds, and I'm pretty sure everybody in the holy family trio was crying just a little.

The father looked at me with an expression of complete wonder. "We thought she was dead."

Mrs. McDonner was rocking back and forth and muttering low like a prayer. "Baby, baby, baby . . ." over and over again.

I swear, there was actually light coming from the booth where they were. I glanced over at Dally, who was a little dewy in the peepers herself.

I smiled at her. "Well, this is something of a happy ending."

She shook her head, avoiding eye contact. "Not quite the end." Then she smiled a little. "But it surely is a lot happier than some might have imagined."

Mrs. McDonner looked up. I guess Cedar had told her I'd found the kid. She locked eyes with mine. I've been paid thousands and thousands of dollars to find things all over the world, and I'm telling you I'd rather be paid with a look like that than all the tea in China. It made the world spin around. It did.

Then she looked over at the policeman. "Can I take her home now?"

He nodded, smiling. "I believe she could go home now if she wanted to."

Ginny nodded. "I'd *like* to go home now."

Mr. McDonner also had quite a look on him. "Mr. Tucker? I'm sayin' that I'm owin' you."

Ginny wiggled off the booth seat. She tossed a look our way. "Thank you."

But it wasn't aimed at me, or at Cedar, or even at Dally. She was looking right at Miss Nina.

Miss Nina was all kinds of avoiding eye contact.

Mrs. McDonner looked down at her daughter, confused. "Are you thankin' Miss Nina for the meal, baby?"

Ginny screwed up her face. "Who's Miss Nina?"

Her mother looked over and nodded her head at the restaurateur. "Miss *Nina.*"

"No." Ginny looked at the old woman, shaking her head. "*Her* name's Christy."

26

ONE, TWO, THREE

Rack focus. Low brass. Every eye in the joint slapped on the figure in the rocker.

Ginny lowered her voice, embarrassed by the obvious turmoil she'd created. "Well, that's what Mr. Wicher said."

Dally was the first one to get her voice box working. "Mr. Wicher told you that this person here . . . was *Christy*?"

The little girl nodded.

"Christy *Rayburn*?"

More nodding.

Dally was talking like a broken record. "The Little Lost Girl?"

"Uh-huh."

"Miss *Nina*?"

The old lady'd finally had enough. "Stop it!"

Big silence.

No wonder Miss Nina had been there in my little

vision quest. No wonder she was lumped in with all the other fictional characters—Miss Nina was just another story-book invention. It was very clear to me in that moment who this woman was. I just had to get her to let it out.

"You're not Christy Rayburn." My voice was taunting. "You couldn't be."

Silence.

"You're not the one," I kept on, "who thought all this up."

Her eyes avoided mine.

"And the one who led poor old Sydney to his grave."

Barely rocking, I could see her face flushing, her jaw grinding.

"You're not the Little Lost Girl."

She was humming, low, to herself.

"Or the kidnapper."

Her humming grew more like a growl.

"Or the murderer."

"Shut up! I never killed nobody." She stopped dead. "Nobody I cared about." She jabbed up a look at me like one of David's poisonous vipers, quick and filled with venom, hissing—with a little lick of the lips.

Mrs. McDonner sat down. I don't think she even knew she'd done it. Her husband was shaking his head. Cedar was clearly flamboozled, I believe that's the technical name for his state of affairs. Dally was just staring at the ghost. I was the only one smiling.

It was clear that I was smiling at the original little girl of Lost Pines. "So you *are* Christy Rayburn."

Cedar was talking almost to himself. "How is that
. . . how is that possible?"

Dally finally smiled too. She was smiling at me.
"Flap, when you tell a story . . ."

". . . I just got to get the punch line in the right
place." I turned back to the old lady. "Feel like telling
us what's really happening here?"

She waved her hand like she was mean-swatting at
a fly. "I don't care."

Cedar was stuck on one note. "How could you be
Christy Rayburn?"

She ignored him and lashed out at the McDonners.
"This town owes me! That land is mine, by rights. I
ought to be the one to make all that money." She
jutted her face at the floor. "Only I couldn't tell."

I lowered my voice. "Tell *what*?"

Her shoulders sagged. "Everything. I couldn't
tell."

Dally's voice was very soothing. "But now you
can."

The old lady was looking away, very downhearted
and downcast and down-whatever-ed. "What's the
difference . . . now?"

Dally tried to get her to look up. "The difference is
. . . that now you can let all the secrets out. You can
open the doors and let everything out. The big one's
already in the open."

I knew Dally was sort of fishing for a response, the
way I did a lot of times, but it had the right effect.
Ms. Rayburn nodded.

She creaked out a long and difficult sigh. I swear it
sounded a little like the cellar door falling open at the

abandoned farm. Then she began to speak, staring down at the wooden floor.

"My daddy used to beat me regular. For nothin'. Got used to it. Stayed away from 'im, mostly. Mama was no help. She stayed away all she could too. I tried askin' her for help. She'd just say, 'Don' make 'im mad, 'at's all.' But ever'thing made him mad. He was just mean as a snake. An' drunk most all the time."

She looked up, right at Cedar. "They all knew. Ever'body in town knew what was goin' on out there. The law knew. Knew about the moonshine too. Never did the first thing about it. People of this town." She said it like a curse.

Mrs. McDonner shook her head like she hadn't heard any of Ms. Rayburn's little speech. "You're my Ginny's great-aunt Christy."

The old lady shook her head too. "Don' want no parta that family. You all never did help me when I was Christy. Just as soon be Miss Nina."

Mrs. McDonner looked at her husband. He looked down. He couldn't have been any more than a boy himself when all that had happened to Christy, but I could tell, all the same, the guilt that was washing his face.

Cedar still wanted answers. "Why didn't you ever tell anybody? Where did you go after the house burned down? When did you come back here? *Why* did you come back?"

Miss Nina smiled. It wasn't pretty. "I come rushin' home one night to show Daddy that jar of fireflies. He lit out after me like a fire truck. Grab the jar. Broke it on my head. Cut me good. Then wailed into me with a poker from the fire under his still. I just run. Hid out till after dark, when I knew he'd be passed out. I just done *had it* with all that. Snuck back. Saw him asleepin' in the still room. Took up a brand from the fire. Set the whole place aflame. Stood by an' watched it burn too. Burn to the ground with both of 'em in it. Good riddance."

Cedar was stone-faced.

Mr. McDonner spoke up. "*You* burned the farm?"

"I did." She began rocking. "Watched it go to the ground."

Cedar's voice was not his own. "Where did you go then?"

She rocked more steadily now. "Had kin up in Mossy Creek. Took me two, three days to walk over to 'em. Told 'em the house burned down with Mama an' Daddy in it. Told 'em it was on account of Daddy's still. Word got out. Ever'body thought it's true. I ask 'em not to tell where I was. Said I was scared. This was back . . . the war was still on. We didn't have no electric lights ner phone ner even indoor wash. It was a different world from today."

Cedar nodded. "And nobody here in Lost Pines knew?"

She sighed. "Not many."

I took a flying guess. "Sydney Wicher knew— something."

She nodded. "We was goin' on bein' sweethearts. I b'lieve he woulda courted me . . . if I'd lived."

I knew what she meant. The whole town thought she was dead. And she didn't mind it that way. It was better for the big town guilt, the collective sense that produces ghosts in the first place.

She was still rocking a little. "I guess I was a wild girl. I didn't stay over in Mossy Creek no longer than I had to. Went down to Marietta, work for that Lockheed. Good job."

Mr. McDonner piped up. "Lotsa people up here in the mountains did that after the war."

Miss Nina stopped rocking finally. "But even after a good long while I *still* couldn't stop thinkin' about how I'd been done. I got to thinkin' about what all this town owed me—what I owed it . . . in retribution. I come back for my revenge."

I was thinking there had to be some kind of psychological name for her particular situation, when it occurred to me what might have been happening with Wicher.

I lit in. "So *you're* the reason Wicher went after Ginny."

She looked at me like I was nuts—a look I'm used to. "No. Sydney saw those two morons get her, and he followed after all on his own." Her voice softened. "He was a good man."

I tried again. "But he married somebody else. Was he one of your revenge objects?"

"Sydney? No. I left town—he thought I was dead for a while there too. He did what he had to. By the time I'd come back to town, I don't believe he even recognized me. Nobody did. You change a lot in thirty years."

I folded my arms. "Took you that long to get back up here?"

She nodded. "Married myself. Had a child. Buried my husband—lung cancer. Child went off." She looked me in the eye. "I had another life. When it was over, I come back here."

Another life. Another story.

Cedar nodded, thinking. "This place been open about twenty, twenty-one years?"

She nodded back.

He looked around. "And in all that time nobody knew who you were?"

She got a shine on her face. "Oh, I made myself known when I had to."

I caught it. "You started most of the rumors and legends about seeing the ghost of the little girl. To keep the guilt alive."

She smiled. I believe I've mentioned the nature of that particular expression, but the temperature in the room dropped noticeably.

I leaned back. "So are you ready to fill us in about the deal with the land and the kidnapping?"

She dropped the smile. "What about it?"

I tilted my head. "For example the two morons you mentioned? They didn't work for Hainey . . ."

Dally got it two seconds before everybody else. ". . . Don't say it."

I had to. I fixed hard on Miss Nina. "They worked for you."

She froze.

I shrugged. "They all but told me already."

She looked away. "Those morons."

I defended them. "They were worried about the kid."

She shook her head, disgusted.

I went on. "So you hired them when you heard Hainey was slingin' around a wad of big dough. And since you figured the land he really wanted was rightfully yours anyway, you had the idea you could get it from the McDonners and then sell it to Hainey; clean up."

She didn't move.

I was hot. "But the thugs bungled it. How did you get in touch with them in the first place, anyway? How does a gal like you know customers like that?"

She tried to decide if maybe she should just stay quiet, or go ahead and spill all her beans into one basket. Then she snorted out a little breath.

"Husband. He run with a rough crowd out of Atlanta. Knew all sorts in those days. These boys—they was referred to me. That's all I can say. An' I'm mighty displeased with 'em."

I understood. "Yeah, because they lost the kid within a half hour of nabbin' 'er."

She shook her head. "Morons I call 'em. Had to make a second plan."

Dally looked at her. "Wicher."

She sighed. "Wicher. He was half gone out his mind anyway. I reckon I'd been in town . . . ten years, maybe, when he happened to be the last one in the place one night. I set down across from 'im. Said, 'Don' I look familiar, Sydney Wicher?' His wife had died, and I allowed as how it was fair for me to reveal myself. But he didn't see it. So I said, 'It's Christy Rayburn, back from the dead.' An' he *looked*. Finally must have seen somethin'. He knowed it was me.

That's when I started in to tellin' 'im I could see the ghost of his wife around 'im." She smiled that smile again. "Really set 'im off."

I shot Dally a look. "So, he knew about you for a long while."

The old witch nodded.

I leaped again. "Fade to day before yesterday. When the boys blew the kidnapping, and you found out it was actually Wicher who'd *helped* Ginny get away, you moved on to what you were just calling your second plan."

She was clear. "Had to."

"And that plan involved getting Wicher to play along, and keep Ginny hiding so you could get a ransom note to the McDonners."

She nodded. "But he didn't like it. Not one bit. Had a soft spot for Ginny. Used to carve 'er dolls an' such."

I nodded. "I've seen one or two."

She picked up the rocking again. "I believe what pushed 'im was my tellin' him that Ginny's parents'd get hurt if she didn't cooperate. That's when he started the nonsense tellin' the child that Christy was helpin' 'er hide, and listenin' to the doll whisper an' all. He just give over to 'is lunacy, I reckon."

Lunacy. From *luna,* meaning "moon." It originally meant something about mental derangement associated with the changing phases of the moon—the same beautiful full moon we'd been having the past few nights to help us in searching for Ginny McDonner. The same full moon that helped Moose catch a bullet.

I asked her about it. "What do you mean, *lunacy*?"

"He just couldn't take it, I reckon—tellin' 'er somethin' that hurt 'er." She lowered her voice by at least half. "Reckon that's why he . . . done what he done."

I blew out a little breath. "Takes quite a conviction to do what he did."

Cedar nodded. "Especially in the heart." Then he looked over at Mrs. McDonner and Ginny. "I'd imagine you all would *really* like to go home now."

Ginny was nearly asleep, and her parents were too stunned by all the events to even answer.

Finally Mr. McDonner picked the little girl up in his arms, and got his wife to her feet. "We'll talk all about this in the mornin'."

I waved at the little nipper. Her eyes were slits, but she smiled.

"G'night, Flap."

"G'night, Ginny."

They rattled out the door. The place seemed empty and quiet indeed.

Cedar took over. "Didn't want to talk about Wicher's . . . apparent suicide . . . not with Ginny right there and everything."

I nodded. "Check."

He went on. "And I thought you'd be interested in the information on the little altar skull."

I sat up. "Oh, right. You got that back."

He nodded. No beating around the bush. "The DNA seems to have matched up with Ms. McDonner's hospital records. It's the remains of her daughter that she miscarried—Ginny's little sister."

Dally dropped her head suddenly. "My God."

I blinked. "They buried her up there?"

Dark nodding.

I shook my head. "Just one more reason why they didn't want to sell, I guess."

Cedar let out a breath. He was very tired.

Dally looked at me. "Mustard used to sing that song, the one you said Ms. McDonner was singing the night of her miscarriage. 'The Cruel Mother.' He used to sing it at family reunions when he was still trying to get his band together. It's the last verse I've got in mind: 'Pretty little girls, one, two, three/One was living, just like me/One was dead and never to be seen/And one, poor girl, was in between.' Ginny's alive, her unborn sister's gone—and Christy Rayburn is in between."

Miss Nina closed her eyes and just kept rocking.

27

FAMILY

Sissy came to the door in a bathrobe with her newborn daughter conked out in her arms. Mustard had
been sleeping most of the time since we'd last seen
him. We didn't want her to, but Sissy insisted on wak-
ing him up to say good-bye.

"He's been asleep near twenty hours all together.
Got up once or twice to eat an' then just went back
down. He needs to get himself *up* now." She reared
back her head. "Mustard!"

She beckoned, we followed. Their living room was
a wreck of presents and leftovers. Dally and I grabbed
what was left of the sofa. Sissy sat in the rocking
chair by the window and looked out.

"Snows meltin'."

Dally looked at her cousin. "Definitely gettin'
warmer. I think spring's here now."

I'm a dope, but I still got the idea they weren't
really talking just about the weather.

Sissy petted her baby with a tenderness that was mystical, then hollered like a stevedore. "Mus*tard*!"

From deep within the hollows of the upstairs lair, a response flew back.

"Huh?"

"Dally an' Flap are here."

"What'd you say?"

"Dally an' *Flap*!"

"What about 'em?"

"They're *here*!"

"Oh."

Big commotion. Sissy turned ever so discreetly toward the window and started feeding little Rose Abernathy.

Staring down at her daughter, Sissy explained it all to us. "They say you have to give 'em breast milk. Formula makes 'em strange."

I nodded, making a face at Dally. "I was a bottle baby."

Sissy smiled. "I rest my case."

Mustard came down the stairs. It was touch and go. One second he seemed in control, the next it looked like he might just come down like an avalanche and pile up at our feet. As luck would have it, he made it to the recliner just in time.

He rubbed his eyes and looked around the room. "Flap?"

I smiled at him. "Get some sleep?"

"Uh-huh."

Dally smiled too. "I think you needed it."

He cleared his throat and shook his head. "You'uns find Ginny yet?"

I looked at Dally, wondering how much I should tell the guy in his somewhat addled state. She shook her head.

I looked back at Mustard. "Yup."

He was satisfied, closed his eyes. "That's good. She okay?"

"Uh-huh."

"Well, then."

Sissy wanted to know a little more.

"Where'd you find her?"

I took a gander at the big boy on the recliner. "Just where he thought we would, more or less."

He opened his eyes. "In the tree hut?"

I shook my head. "Did you know there was a cellar on the property, at the abandoned farm?"

"Really?"

I nodded. "She was down there when we found her."

Sissy looked back at her daughter. "An' she's back home now?"

Dally smiled. "Back home."

Mustard stared hard at the floor. "Reckon why she run off like that?"

I took a deep breath. Dally shrugged.

I started. "I don't know how much you care to know, but the basics are that she was kidnapped. Then she escaped with the help of Sydney Wicher, and *then* she hid out for a while because she thought her parents were in danger because Wicher *said* they were." I glanced over at Sissy and lowered my voice. "And now Wicher's dead and Ginny's safe and warm."

Sissy and Mustard shot me a look out of a rifle.

Mustard sat up. "Wicher's *dead*?"

Dally nodded. "They think he might have killed himself."

Mustard nodded. "I'll be."

Sissy was very calm. "Mustard always said he'd die by his own hand, that man."

I looked at him. "Really?"

Mustard nodded. "You know how I get these feelin's sometimes." He leaned over closer to us. "He shot hisself in the heart, didn't he?"

Dally shook her head in slow wonder. "Close enough."

I looked at him. "What do you think are the chances of you an' me bein' related in some odd way, bud?"

He leaned back. "We *all* jus' one great big ol' family, Flap."

Dally looked down. "There's more."

Sissy turned her head a little our way. "About who kidnapped 'er in the first place?"

Dally smiled. "Sort of."

Mustard rubbed his eyes. "An' *why*? What's there to kidnap little Ginny McDonner for?"

I jumped in. "They own the Rayburn place, the McDonners do. They own that whole mountain."

Mustard was very surprised. "Really?"

Dally tossed her hand like she knew everything in the world. "They don't like to talk about it."

I supplied more information. "Ms. McDonner is related to the family somehow."

Mustard nodded. "That's right. The mother *was* a

Day. Wouldna thought the McDonners 'ud get the land, though."

Sissy rocked very gently, had an explanation. "Not no Rayburns *up* this way. Closest we got's over in Mossy Creek—an' they don't want a *thing* to do with this part of the mountains."

Dally pressed on. "So that guy Hainey that's been around here for a while?"

Mustard settled in his chair. "That one that's wantin' to buy all the land up here for some business or other?"

Dally nodded. "Uh-huh. He wanted Black Pine Mountain."

"So why didn't he just get it?"

I jumped in again. "They wouldn't *sell*. Guess why?"

Mustard looked at me. "Too many ghosts."

Well—right. I raised my eyebrows. "In essence."

Dally added, "And guess what skull that is we found up there."

Mustard got wide-eyed. "Christy Rayburn!"

"Nope." I shook my head. "The unborn sister of Ginny McDonner."

Mustard's expression changed radically. "That poor little thing. That's where they buried 'er? Up there?"

"That's right." Then I let the last arrow fly. "But speaking of Christy, guess what about her."

Sissy guessed this time. "She's buried up there too."

I let a second of silence set the stage for the big

announcement. "Not in the least. Christy Rayburn is still alive."

Big reaction. Mustard fell forward and stomped on the floor. Sissy jerked around so quick, it upset the baby, who started wailing.

Dally and I could barely contain ourselves.

Dally had to have the last word. "It's Miss Nina. Miss Nina is Christy Rayburn. The Little Girl of Lost Pines has, in *fact,* been haunting you all for all these years—from over at the *restaurant.*"

There was much disbelief and 'Oh, my God' and all manner of incredulity before things calmed down again. Then the atmosphere kind of settled back and the baby went to sleep and Sissy started yawning.

I figured this news would be enough to fire conversations in Lost Pines and Oglethorpe family reunions for the next ten or maybe even twenty years, but the time for us to take our leave of this particular adventure had come.

We told them how Cedar had carted the old bat off. She actually spit on the ground when he put her into his police-mobile. A couple of hundred years earlier she would have been a candidate for burning at the stake. As it was, Cedar figured she'd spend the rest of her days in a nice home—one that was supported by our tax dollars. More head shaking and allowing as how life was just the strangest thing ever.

We probably bid as fond a farewell as I've ever personally been a part of. What with the hugging and the back patting and the one-more-no-really-just-one-more look at the baby, it probably took the better part of an hour. Leaving like adults, Dally and I used to call it when we were kids. Kids say good-bye and split. Adults say good-bye, then talk some more, then say good-bye and make all types of observations about the trip and the weather and such, and then say good-bye and start to plan the *next* trip, and then . . . you get the picture.

Dally understood when I told her I had to stop by the hospital to see what was what with the Moose. Even after all the weird revelations over at Miss Nina's I'd remembered to fill up a grocery sack with some very crispy fried okra. Just the thing for a gun-shot wound.

Moose was asleep after his surgery. The bullet went right through his side. Messed up some muscle and a little of his guts, but I figured he had plenty of both to spare. And Fedora assured me that what he'd said was true, he actually *had* been shot plenty worse than that.

Fedora himself was in a reflective mood. He knew that he and the big guy were going to the joint for kidnapping, but all his questions were about Ginny. Was she all right? Were her parents all right? Did she get some dinner?

Then he looked at me and said a strange thing.

"That Miss *Nina* broad? Some people never grow up."

I asked him what he was talking about.

He looked deep into the corner of the room, where it was dark and calm. "After a certain age a person really ought to quit with the blamin' other people for the way things turned out, and take it on the chin like everybody else. A kid'll go on all day about how it

was somebody else's fault, but an adult person
oughta straighten up an' fly right. So she had it tough
when she was a kid. Who didn't, if you don't mind
my askin'? Eventually you just have to stop blamin'
your old man or your old lady or all the other people
that done you dirt. Ya just got to move on down the
line."

I thought it was quite a speech, coming from a guy
who was moving on down the line to a federal insti-
tution for kidnapping a minor.

We spent a while debating the Wicher-suicide issue. He couldn't get it right in his mind that a guy
could feel so guilty and lonely and sad that he'd actually drill a hole in his own heart.

One of Duffie's boys came around after a while
and told me that visiting hours were over. He was
actually very gentle about it, I thought. I handed over
my bagful of okra, tipped my hat, and shoved off.

Dally'd been chatting it up with a couple of the
nurses. They all hushed up pretty solid when I came
around. I figured they'd clammed up on account of
they thought I was another hood like the two guys I'd
just been visiting. Dally just smiled, and we trundled
out the emergency-room door and into the light of
the moon.

28

LA GRÂCE DIEU

It was going for midnight by the time we were in the car and headed down the road south, back toward Atlanta—back home. The air was very clean, and the night was perfect. Not a cloud in the sky. The roads were completely free of snow, but there was plenty on the side of the roads for making with the picturesque view-ology under a big full moon.

We shuttled down the road a comfy forty miles per, and rounded the turn right there by the McDonner place, when wouldn't you know: We saw a bright flash of red in the road right in front of us.

I slammed on the brakes and we shushed for a moment, but we managed to stay out of the damaged corn area in general.

I put my arm out to Dally. "You okay?"

She peered into the darkness. "What was *that*?"

I got out of the car. There wasn't a thing on the road in either direction. I was just about to make an astute observation about the nature of ghostly objects in general, when an eerie noise came from the side of the road.

I zipped my head around.

Then the voice. "I'm all right."

David's head popped up. A second later he stood in the ditch by the side of the road trying to get his bicycle up. "This damn thing."

I went over to help him. Red reflectors. Maybe a dozen of the things.

I touched one. "These things just saved your life."

He was disgusted. "I don't know why I ride this *bike*. I can barely make it up the small hills, and I always have to *walk* it up the mountain. Doctor said it'd be good for my cholesterol, but it surely is bad for my temperament." He tossed me a look. "You want it?"

I pulled my head back. "Me? I like my cholesterol. I want all I can get. Plus, a thing like this? Riding a bike? It'd mess with my image to no end."

He sighed. Then he collected himself. "You and Ms. Oglethorpe leaving?"

"Uh-huh."

He leaned over and waved at Dally. "Hey."

She waved back.

He shook his head. "Heard all about it. Who would *ever* have thought Miss Nina . . ."

I shook my head too. Then—and I don't know what made me do it—I stuck out my hand. "Just wanted to say . . . something about how much I got out of your service, odd as it was."

He took my hand and smiled. "Who can explain the ways of faith?"

I nodded. "Not me."

"But you got something out of it."

"I did."

"Something that helped bring a little girl home."

"I guess."

"Well, then." He gathered up his primitive method of locomotion. "You've done quite well. Finish the wine, and have a safe trip home."

And he was on his bike and around the corner, flashing all kinds of red around the road.

I shot a look to Dally. "Not one word about *this* coincidence."

She smiled. "I would never dream—"

"Let's get going."

We were well down the road, a nice tape of Vivaldi's *Spring* in the cassette player, before I felt like asking, "What'd he mean by, 'Finish the wine, then go home?' I mean, what do you think he meant?"

She was looking out the window. "How'd he even know we *had* wine?"

I nodded. "That's right." I squinted. "What've we got? Like, half a bottle still left from the church *plus* another full one?"

She looked at me. "Yup."

I started scouting the side of the road. "Then let's finish the bottle we started; make with the roadside picnic—like you wanted to in the first place."

One glass each. Well under the legal limit. I never drive if I've had more than half a bottle—I might have mentioned I'm not that fond of driving anyway, so any excuse would do to keep me off the roads. But we had to finish the ceremony, didn't we?

It wasn't too long before I spotted one of those roadside-overlook jobs. It was really just a place to pull off and have a gander at the valley below and the wide expanses of wide expanse. There was a concrete picnic table. Dally fetched what was left of the open bottle.

I poured. "I'm really glad you remembered to snag this when we went back to the church for your car going over to Miss Nina's."

She turned her head. "I didn't get this. I thought you got it. You're the one who can't live without this stuff."

I looked at the bottle. "I didn't get it."

She only had to ponder a second more. "*That's* how Dave knew we had the wine. He must have put it back in my car."

I picked up my glass. "I didn't even know he was there."

She shrugged. "Me neither."

I sipped. "So . . . what was he doing up there, skulking around and not making himself known?"

She looked out at the view. "I don't know."

I looked at the side of her face. "Show a little enthusiasm. Maybe this whole deal is a little more complicated than we thought."

She shrugged.

I took a deep breath. I wanted to pursue the last little drop of mystery, but I could tell Dally herself had other fish to fry, so I skipped the minor stuff and went to the heart of the matter. "Sugar, you've been on the verge of something since we *started* this trip. You said you brought the vino for a special purpose." I looked around, tried for the charming smile. "So here we are. Moonlit night. Good wine. The gig up here is solved—over and done with. I'm all ears. Spill."

She nodded, took another fair-sized sip. No eye contact. "Okay." Big pause, little sigh. "Look, when I was down in Savannah, last month?"

"Yeah?"

"I had a little trouble."

I sat up. "What kind of trouble?"

"Had to . . . go to the hospital."

I set down my glass. "Jesus, Dally. What for? Why don't you *tell* me these things? Damn."

She took another sip. "I'm *telling* you."

"So *what for?*"

"That's not really important. Turned out to be nothing, but I found out something while I was there that I've still got to think over."

I was absolutely baffled.

She looked at me, finally. "I don't think I . . . I may not be able to have kids."

I leaned forward on the table and stared into her eyes. "I had no idea you *wanted* to."

She smiled a little. "Yeah. Me neither—until I found out I might not be able to. Then, you know . . . suddenly it's, like, an *issue*."

"Are they sure? I mean, sure that you *can't?*"

She took in a deep breath. "Well, no."

"So . . . that's what you want to talk about?"

She looked away again. "Not really . . . not yet. I just wanted you to know, is all. For some reason."

More baffled than ever. "Okay, then, what's the wine and the picnic for?"

She sipped. More nodding. "Well . . . I just wanted to tell you—I think I'm going to be gone for a little while." Big sip, still avoiding eye contact. "Maybe hit Europe. I hear they've got a lot of nice stuff in Parisfrance."

She said it just like that, like it was one word. Parisfrance.

I looked out at the night. "Yeah. You know how fond I am of most things French."

She nodded. "Yeah."

I didn't feel like explaining what the news was doing to my mood. "How long you plan on being gone?"

"Oh . . . not long."

"Just a kind of getaway."

"Yeah."

I picked up my glass again. "Well—you *have* been working pretty hard lately, what with getting the new club going and everything. You could use what the straights call a vacation."

That made her smile a little. "A *what*?"

"Yeah. It's an American invention where you *don't* actually work all the time."

"*Vacation*, huh? Like the sound of it."

I tossed back a goodly portion of my glass. "But don't stay gone too long. You know how I languish in your absence."

Another laugh. "Yeah. You don't do squat when I'm not around, do you?"

"I barely move."

She finished her glass. "Okay, it's a deal. I'll only stay gone as long as I absolutely have to."

I finished my glass. I reached out without thinking and clutched her hand a minute. "What a fine, *fine* woman you are. And look—you never can tell, right? I mean, medicine—it's more guesswork than science most of the time, don't you think?"

She squeezed back a little harder than I thought she would, and for a change I had the impulse to say something to *her* that I didn't.

We finished the wine in silence, and the moon spilled everywhere. If you'd have taken a deep enough breath, I think you could have smelled spring coming.

The rest of the drive back to Atlanta we finished out Vivaldi's *Four Seasons,* Miles Davis's *Kind of Blue*, and Van Morrison and the Chieftains' *Irish Heartbeat.* Dally didn't make it past Vivaldi. She was sound asleep. I turned down the treble a little, so as not to wake her up.

Now, a guy like me—who doesn't do much when a certain fine, fine woman isn't around—has a lot of time for idle reading. This is how I know about a guy named Charles Lamb. He was some kind of English writer who was pals with Wordsworth. Lamb wanted to get married, I gathered, to some belle name of Alice, but she up and married somebody else instead. He was not happy. So he's sitting in his armchair one night, and he suddenly has a vision of two little ghostly kids standing beside him. They tell him, "We are not of Alice, nor of thee, nor are we children at all. We are nothing; less than nothing, and dreams. We are only what might have been . . . ," and so forth. He wrote about it in something called *Dream-Children*.

So as I was driving down the highway at midnight, when the hands of the clock were pressed together like they were praying, and Dally was fast asleep beside me, I developed another theory about ghosts. Maybe they weren't all psychological manifestations of some kind of guilt after all. Maybe, sometimes, a ghost was an echo—an echo of longing, or loss.

Or maybe, if the moon is right, and spring is in the air, and you have a little luck on your side—a ghost could just possibly be the promise of a happier ending than you might imagine.